This Rendezvous

with

Life

collected poetry and prose

by

Diane Porter Goff

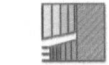

Dreamsplice
Christiansburg, Virginia

For Larkin, who brings the Light.

DPG

Also by Diane Porter Goff:

Riding the Elephant: an Alzheimer's Journey

Contents

Poetry

Kin	7
This Natural World	23
The Big C	35
Two by Two	47
Spirit	57
Poems for Children	71

Prose

Senator	79
John Epps and Miss Bessie	85
Caboose	91
Trip to Seychelles	109
Blue	115
Meeting Kan	125

Kin

Bath
Nap
February Incubus
For Baby Larkin
Goddess Mother Moon
Into the Woods
For Larkin
Dancing
Flight
The Salt Daughter
Muse

Bath

I kneel to bathe Mama in my tub
her small body sits upright
legs stuck straight out   like a child's

I sluice water over the pearl string of her spine
the pulled skin where the soft breast   should be
folded over and sewn
like the thick   crooked
hem of a skirt

she leans in with a glare
"are you kin to me?"
I cannot answer   grief
has my tongue

I lather her hair into soft peaks   meringue
on pie
cupping her chin   I tilt her head back
and pour
shampoo runs over her
like milk foam

her eyes grow dull
arms lie still   misshapen
under the water   the washcloth
floats
a discarded flower

her body   slick as a newborn
her head in my palm
heavy   as dread
the tap drips
a bird screams outside   the window

I pour and pour   I cannot
stop
it seems I will always kneel here
knees aching
sweat beading me
love   a hand
at my throat

Nap

we never knew we would lie down like this
my older sister and I
napping in the torpor of a hot afternoon in Egypt
while fifteen stories below the Cairo traffic seethes
and air beats dust into trailing veils
of the women   the smell
of shisha rises from the lolling clumps of men
flame trees spread umbrellas of rich orange
over boxed stations where men with guns
stare heavily at us in the evening's cool
when we walk by

so far from the summer naps of childhood
upstairs in the farmhouse our grandfather built
just outside our southern town
after Mama closed the door
sometimes we slept   drowsing
into the sound of each other's breath
waking with damp necks and entangled limbs

other times we would cavort
jumping on the squeaking bed   our heads
rising one by one
into the curve of the long mirror on the wall
our hair aloft in bright crowns   our grins suspended
in the heavy air

we would kneel at the window looking down
the wide yard at the pink beautybush   frowsy with heat
sending up its scent
the long-handled pump in the concrete block
where we coaxed up cool buckets of water
on sweaty nights   dotted with fireflies
and the laughter of cousins

if Mama also napped   her back rolled up between us
my sister passed me folded notes above her head
"I love you. Signed, Beverly" in her finest second-grade hand
and I   my fingers tingling with happiness
would place my X beside her name
and pass the paper back

the haunting drone of the call to prayer floats in from the city's
minarets
and I wake   a nameless dread fluttering in my throat
my sister sighs and turns and sleeps again
our breaths take on the same rhythm   the same song
after years of other melodies with husbands children friends
lying here in a land we do not yet understand
our note lifts me to that past refrain
of liquid summer ease   undaunted
by the passage of the world
my sister lies beside me   sleeping

*[Published in **Artemis**]*

February Incubus

All throughout February
they sit with their chairs
pushed back, dreaming
of Florida. I bring brochures:
alligators wrestlers in pink tights,
eels in plastic tanks,
fake showboats that run
the canals of Fort Lauderdale.

It is the sun they crave.

In his youth, my father
rode standing up in the saddle
down through the main street
of that mountain town
racing with the other boys.

In her youth, my mother
laughed, hopping quicksand
to reach that wild
swamp flower she loved.

Outside the dark clouds
catch and tear in the bare
February branches. They doze.
Their feet twitch and run
in the edges of their dreams.

It is another sun
they crave.

*[Published in **Jam Today**: Issue 6 1978]*

For Baby Larkin

in the window frame
a gibbous moon   signs its chop
in the corner of the sky

I have come to listen to you
       breathe

you wake and I take up the bundle of you
questing eyes   silken belly   tiny
fingers and toes
you smell like
       home
a home I never knew
to imagine

you nurse and in the night
I am feeding you
       light

my dark beauty
where have we walked before and why
your little curdy tongue flashes   white
in the moonlight

Goddess Mother Moon

Goddess

phosphorescent loose coil slipping back to reveal
the double egg
nestled in the curve of the crescent
parthenogenesis   we clone   goddess I spawn you and you me
you licking the caul from my eyes
my breath singing in your throat
we are complete   whom shall we call?

we call sunrider from the east
digger from the south
snotboy from the west
redworm from the north
to get babies   to get poems

the wise crone moves upon us
where her horned eyebrows sprout   hearts open
serpents spew forth   soft eternal umbilicus

Mother

mother   your hazel eyes the only thing holding me to earth
as you kneel beside me in the screaming ambulance
clutching the jar with the shimmering cranberry jelly clot
blood everywhere
the doctor who said "Take her on to St. Judes." You lifted
off the floor
said "You will take her now!"
all night I watched the decoration of your fingers on his lapels
tiny red dragons with a dragons fiery breath

Moon

on the day of the night of the blue moon
I bleed again   the wise wound   she who bleeds but does not die
not the taboo   the curse   unclean
but a power so strong it would shake down the sweat lodge
whirl planets   displace skulls   tell the caribou when to come

moon as you draw out my magic tides
so I draw you down
to meet behind the seventh star
spinning liquid infusion   syrup mead
mother may I?   Yes   a giant leap?   Yes
we carry the world   the stuff of life
goddess mother moon

*[Published in **Artemis**]*

Into the Woods

I'll always have that day
when my daughter and I went into the woods
with our sleds
she, twelve, innocent to the hormones
approaching her like an avalanche
to toss her through the surges of adolescence
I, forty-six, oblivious to the menopausal whirlpool
about to pull me under.

we went into the forest, that glittering day of snow
and played on the edge of the world
zigzagging through trees
down daredevil slopes
crashing into giant drifts
spinning out onto the frozen creek
laughing, falling, getting up
eating snow
two animals in simple skins.

soon after that
deep in her belly, a different kind of knowing
rose through her body
pouring gold
to the edges of her skin
deep in my belly, a sheen of vigor
gave way
and a different kind of knowing
drove through my body
and thickened my flesh.

we slipped into our new roles
like slipping into coats
hers a slinky mink, exuding a troubled musk
sliding away from my fingers at every grasp
mine a tattered muskrat from the back of my mother's closet
something she had never shown me
how to wear.

For Larkin

My pen stopped
fingers numb on the keys

the red flags flying high and bright
my daughter's eyes asking for answers
that can only come from her

she has become small
and I am afraid
dread soaks my body
as I watch her navigate

this broken man
this beaten boy
has thrown his life over her
like a twisted net
snarling her thoughts
battering her wide heart

she watches
she knows the way out
her feet falter on the path
but she is walking
walking the walk
of her life.

June, 2019

Dancing

On the thick, Moroccan rug
in my sister's finely appointed apartment.
we dance, my daughter, sister, niece and I,
to "Boot Scootin' Boogie" by Brooks and Dunn.
Fifteen stories below,   Cairo unfurls
her dark night scarf, aglitter with sequins,
the slick ribbon of the Nile meandering the edge.

We dance our memories
we shimmy and stomp and clap
in memory of Mama,
who, deep in Alzheimer's,
danced with us in the mornings to this song
swaying   tapping her narrow feet
swiping the air with outstretched hands
cutting her blue eyes at us as though to say,
"This is nothing but fun!"

We dance our sorrow
we dance for the ragged old man we saw
pissing against the stones at the walled tombs
where he lives with his family
in The City of The Dead.

We shake out our hair
For the elder woman in the black chador
who resides at the back
of the parking garage with her husband,
their pallets rolled up in the corner.

We dance for the blind widow
perched on the steps of the Coptic Christian Church,
her grimy palm turned perpetually up
the milky eyes almost lost in the puffed, wrinkled face.

We dance our loss
we dance in memory of Daddy,
that mountain man,
that bulwark of our lives   who would get up and clog dance
in the middle of the floor
"Chicken in the Bread Pan Peckin' Up Dough

Flight

In haunting rhythm   the owl
drops her hollow notes into the rise of darkness
outside your window
and I rush to sit beside your bed   praying
she has come to bear you away on her spotted back,

away from this place where your breath whimpers and cries
and you have lost the syllables of your own name,
where bedsores etch your flesh
down to the white shine of bone.

Morning light   the owl flown
any hope of mercy pinned
in her cruel beak.
Your eyes beckon.   "Please," you whisper,
your voice soft as down.

Perhaps the pillow   underneath your head
the one with the white casing
we bought together that spring day
for my trousseau,
you saying   mother to daughter,
"I want you to have a white wedding night."
and laughing with joy   that we could
speak so plainly.

If I positioned it just right
centered above your face
when I pressed down
its two sides   would rise like wings,
the lace on one edge
a scalloped fringe of feathers.

If I could fold up my heart
and tuck it away   for just those few moments,
perhaps that pillow bird
could be your ride   out of here.

The Salt Daughter

She rises from the deepest part of the ocean
the place   where the blind things dwell
the place where she spent   her time
of blinding

On her lips the bitter taste of salt
of sweat
of tears
of blood

The smell of salt
infuses her skin

In her hair
the shine of salt
glistens in the moon's path

She rises streaming sea stars and sky stars
she rises to her Self as a star
she rises to re member all of us
salt
she rises to re member all of us
stars.

Muse

After some had died and some had gone away
I pressed my face into the bitter grass
and called the Muse
She did not come
but I saw her moving against the shadow of the mountain
her hair trailing
like smoke

I went into the room under the beveled eves
and lay in my mother's last bed
I lifted my arms and prayed to the Muse
She did not come
but I heard her voice seep into the corners of the room
like blood

I walked to the house where my sister once lived
carrying memories in my arms as I had carried her children
I knelt to the Muse
She did not come
but the taste of sorrow gathered in my throat
like ash

I waded into the river
where my father had taught me to hook the carapace
of a hellgrammite and cast into the tumbling froth
I cried out for the Muse
She did not come
but the smell of water closed over my heart
like iron

I climbed the maple where my daughter
had placed her nimble foot into the rope swing loop
to arc out into the golden sun
I beseeched the Muse
she did not come
but I felt her touch splinter my spine
like ice

I stood on the hill where my husband and I held hands
and watched forty shooting stars spin across the sky
I whispered to the Muse
She did not come
But I felt her breath against my limbs
like dust

I sat before the mirror and stared
and did not turn my face away
from my own loneliness
until I had seen all the world's peoples
reflected in my eyes

And the Muse came
and wrapped me in her wings
like the center of a rose
and when my tears were spent
I took up my pen

This Natural World

Morning Garden
Clear Cut
Daffodils
Fractured
Crow Call
Flowering
Summer Rhapsody

Morning Garden

The sun sings
on the bright lip of the world
the garden wakes from
its night dream

something scurries
something alights
something leans
the mystery of the garden
settles over me
like grace

the silken throat of the lily
whispers today's secret
as the bee takes suck
her feet festooned with pollen

attar of skunk
bedevils the crisp pink rose
the crow
drops like a dark kite onto
the white pebble path

a breeze conducts the choir
of the grasses
the trail beckons with
fragrant twists
and succulent turns

frowsy seed heads stir
with my breath
blackberries
buxom and roly-poly
tumble under my fingers

I must touch
everything
I must breathe
everything

morning has come
and I open my heart
to take sacrament

Clear Cut

the cloud lays its soft palm
over the brow of the mountain

howling machinery silences the wind
slopes shudder
with the drum of falling trees
the tortured hill   festers
with chain saw oil   tobacco plugs
spit out   flattened cans
plastic bags   food wrappers

bewildered roots claw the air
the gutted spring
has lost her way
torn up berry thickets   streak
the mud with purple tears

deer   stumble
to find their beds   turkey flocks scatter
from the dead hen twisted
in a tree branch   in the lee
of a hill the fox den
sits empty   its cache
of bones
still stuck with bits of flesh   and hair

the red tailed hawk and her mate
spiral round and round
with strangled   cries
and disappear

the cloud lays its soft palm
over the brow of the mountain

Daffodils

I can see him across the field
Moving with the dark bulk of his tractor
Always moving toward me
And then away
Coming so close that my heart starts up
But always turning the big tractor
Back to the field again
And it seems he will never come in to me
That I shall never know him again
That I shall always have to watch him
Moving away from me across the field

This morning he came with daffodils
His arms full of them at the door
His wrists flashed brown in the flower's yellow
He thrust them toward me with a quick sure motion
And some had fallen to the floor
As I took them with my arms he laughed
And his teeth closed upon one another carefully
Like those of a female animal
Closing upon the neck-skin of her young

Then without speaking he went out to plow
Going round and round the field
Always turning his head toward me and then away

The daffodils have settled deep
Into the white windowsill
The sun has entered them and burst them
With its own rich warm yellow
And their hot heavy fragrance permeates me
Permeates the room
Till I feel sick and can no longer move
I can only sit and watch him
Going round and round the field.

*[Published in **Jam Today**, Issue 6: 1978]*

Fractured

To my garden
to gather the healing daze
of sun and shadow,
to steep my wound in the tonic of the Mother.

Come, billowy seed heads, stroke
away the black bruise that sleeves
my arm like an ugly tattoo.

Nasturtium, bring your orange fire to cauterize
the pain, searing the ache into
the bloom of a scar.

Tissue-thin pink petals of fall azalea,
weave the layers of my flesh as gauze,
coming together in the perfect bouquet.

Oh green, green fern, affix your delicate pattern
onto the bone, coax your exact symmetry to remember,
to knit,
to stitch, to mend.

Gaudy beautyberry, lay you down in the muddy rivers
of my marrow. Your bohemian purple pearls
ululating a clarion call - wake up, wake up - resounding throughout the
cells.

And the fall afternoon sun,
dancing like a gypsy in the colored leaves,
inscribing on the body of the earth the hieroglyphic
that mends us all
together.

Crow Call

Crows come to my call   sailing
in like dark leaves
falling through trees
dart   at bread and apple curls
flung on pebble path
dip bread in birdbath
smothered with leaves
scold and peck   to break
the curls against a branch

crow lights on live power pole
BANG   drops as a black stone
my husband and I rush to the body   limp
beak open   tip of grey tongue
bead eyes wet

we wait for others   to notice
to circle
to mourn
to only be curious
nothing

we stretch the cooling body out
with pins
on cardboard
take photographs
the ragged feather fringe like unfinished bits
of poems

at night I dig out my black candles
used for spells
light a candle for crow
on my altar
under the rough carved wooden statue
of a nature goddess
from South America
her pointy breasts
the leaves at her base remind me
of wings

I light another candle to celebrate
the element of   sudden
demise

Flowering

beating up from the tap root   the pulse
forms the bud
raindrop slides into the tiny crevice
unfolding a petal   the finger
of the sun
twirls open the full poppy array-
pink fan with a purple heart
bees nuzzle the sex
stamen pistil   piercing
the membrane   emerging glorious
lapping the air
pollen drifts in a golden swarm

A bead of nectar quivers at the tip
reflecting the sparkling disk
of the day
A bird cries a note of longing
from deep in the bush

the poem
takes its place in the world

Summer Rhapsody

sweet watermelon juice chin run down
to riotous dance in the dirt with all our toes
seeds spilt like jewels
tremble and burst
sap shooting upward just underneath the bark

a sundog wiggles above gap mountain

bodies unfold cells to receive heat
bountiful smell of sweat
the salt-lick wound of winter   pulsing to light

green lie down with leaves
green the fern hairs of this turning body
to roast in the spit juice of the sun
peeling back the fingers to find green
summer greenwave break into us
smashing full heat into breastbone   thigh and shank

shaking loose a thousand petals
perfume from a thousand flowers
bloodroot, cinquefoil, pinks
bluebells, mad-dog-skullcap
toad lily trillium flax
the pink bruised fruit of bleeding heart

sink down in warm wet   the quiet
tiny scratch of ankle bracelets against skin
slide of river reeds over bright rocks
burble of children laughing underwater

a sundog capers over salt pond mountain

ice cream cone lick of shoulders
the backs of knees
smell of freckles on the skin
we open   flood upon the land   the sky
in that most ancient,
new and bursting ecstasy

the hot juice hissing
in the cauldron   of the belly
of summer

April

Spring pops
Flower tops!

The Big C

Seed
Galahad
Tonsured
Drip
Tether
Avatar
Instinct
Salud
Return

Seed

Oval and slippery   just under the skin
supraclavicular lymph node   the click
of Google   tumor or infection in right breast
or lung.

Already today winter has me by the scruff   spread
eagle   facedown on the rug
hard bit belly   the ache
of dead leaf duff in the yard   hollow birds at the feeder
koi crying against the skim of pond ice
dried grass scratching to get in.

My feet dangle
finding no purchase.

If you soak a seed in water
it may sprout   tendril sticking up periscope-like
the slow uncurling of the leaves
while roots map the body like a diagram   of dread.

Like a secret
no one wants to hear.

*[Published in **Artemis** XXIII 2016]*

Galahad

I make you welcome.
You derive from trees, after all.
Taxotere from the Pacific yew,
Topotecan from Tibet's xi shu tree.
I kneel, supplicant,
Where dark roots finger earth.

Trees I can manage.

In the drip room
My veins roll away from the needle.

Threaded at last
You enter, flushing hot.
A knight in burnished silver,
You gallop through my body,
Burning out cancer cells with the tip of your lance,
The grate of your gold-plumed helmet
Hiding a mystery face.

The following days you drag me into dullness
A drab half-twilight where we lie intertwined
In some distant stable room
Fit only for ailing animals.

I awake to pain, sirens, doctors with worried eyes.
I learn you have non-discriminatory tendencies.
Your lance flails everywhere.
You are out for blood,
My blood.

In drug's suede sleep
I pull open the grate across your face.
You are Gollum, gargoyle with a pointed tongue.
You slouch through my body,
Sucking, wallowing in my marrow,

Popping my white cells like candy.
You squat, knees akimbo, on the crown of my head,
Reaching into my fontanel,
Numbing my brain with your scaly hands.

Crippled by your touch,
I watch the trees from my bedroom window.
Spring burgeons the leaf,
The sap swells turgid just beneath the bark,
The branches soar up,
Up to the zenith of the sky.
I know them, these trees.

The tulip poplar pushes its orange flame blossoms to the sky,
Yellow pollen trembling in the cups.
The fir sprouts tiny chartreuse wings on the tips of its branches.
The ancient silver maple,
That has outlived the arborists' guess by fifteen years,
Is entreating the wind into its thick branches
To catch and spin its whirligig seeds
Into a shower of delight.

Tonsured

I knew a woman who shaved her head
Releasing all outer beauty
To walk a spiritual path.

My red hair, my only vanity.

Now I sit in my kitchen
Caped in a black plastic garbage bag,
My husband looming with his clippers.
My sister flanks me
And my daughter peers from the kitchen counter
Courtesy of Skype.

I tug out a handful
To show the video camera
That it is, indeed, time.

We take the high road,
Laughing, joking, singing songs from "Hair"
While the clippers buzz my head like bees
And the hanks fall in soft pats to the floor.

The job done
I put up my hands
To feel a soft, slick ball
Between my fingers,
The ears like two obtuse handles.
A hairless newborn
With the fontanel closed tight,
Life pulsing underneath.

Drip

In the drip room
Just before Thanksgiving
I chat with two old queens
About different ways to make good gravy.
I visited their orchid greenhouse down a long winding road,
A colorful breath of tropical oasis in mid-winter.

The young lawyer who always wears makeup and earrings,
Who loves the color blue,
Grows thinner every week,
Shows off her new wig,
Tells us she has always wanted to be a blonde.

The backwoods couple, the man with the ZZ Top beard,
Snores in his mountainous belly with his suspenders straining.
His wife, sharp and feral as a fox,
Perches on a chair in front of him,
Her eyes never leaving his face as she tells us over and over
That he will be OK.

When the little boy,
Maybe six or seven, his shoelaces trailing,
Comes in with his mother
We all fall silent, watching to see which one's arm
Will get the needle.

Tether

(for Larkin)

Life charms unravel
The stitches picked, the thread rotten,
Hanging askew.

Bedclothes hiss around my ankles.
The air boils,
Tea bleeds in the cup.
Darkness bleats in my throat.

Pain whittle, whittle:
Jackknife, steak knife, cleaver, bludgeon.

The moon spins backwards.
Floodwaters breach the windowsill.

It is only my daughter's soft form beside me,
Her steady hand on my arm, stroking,
Stroking,
That tethers me to all I knew
Or want to know.

Avatar

A wolf has come to stay,
by invitation   or choice
the dream is unclear
only she settles her sleek limbs
with entitlement
onto the end of my sad bed
she watches me with keen eyes
silver ruff springing   from her neck
haunches coiled
inky toenails dark   and wet
ruby tongue glistening
the smell of wild
coming off her   like smoke.

She is how I will devour
the summer days   as I once did
loping   through the tall grasses
plush seed heads brushing my skin
entering the river again   and again
to tumble in the currents,
swimming to the far bank
pulling myself up to sun on the flat   hot rocks.

I will lavish myself
with the sweet   sharp   sandy smells
that heat pulls from the earth
dozing the night in my cool earth wallow
call of the owl   the mummer of insects
pleasures rocked in the cradle of the moon.

I will follow the tracks of animals
deep into the brush
where Nature keeps her mysteries
the berry   the blossom   the springs
I will push my muzzle into cold
and drink like I am famished
famished for   The Mother's feast.

Instinct

(for Richard)

The dark is overtaking us,
We two on this blood island,
The hospital belly rumbling and clicking,
Tubes and needles.

Beyond all the little kindnesses
Our animal body scents the truth:
Snouted nurses with their glittering teeth,
The doctor, his hand on my wrist
Like a paw.

All those years ago,
Your hot flame drew me like the moth.
Though I singed,
I also kindled.
Life has burnished us.

They herd the door.
The snarl leaps into your voice,
Claws and pricked ears,
Thickened viscera.
You beat back the dark
Like the pulsing breath
Of some feral god.

Your palm is coarse.
Amid the bloody footprints
You twirl me round.
I circle once, twice
And fall into an illumined sleep,
My tail across my nose.

Salud

That night I feel my strength returning in bits,
In tiny taps along my spine,
A humming that wakens me from sleep.
"Is that you?" I whisper,
Afraid the chemo will whisper back, "Nope, still me."

But the only answer is hope
That rises like helium in my bones,
Pulls me from my bed
Through the dim kitchen
Out the back door
Into the warm yard
Where a big, round orange moon
Sticks her head up over the horizon,
As bald as I am bald.
I watch her come barreling up,
Stand underneath her chubby face
And my soul goes wide
As she is wide.

At the top of the sky
She turns silver,
Drops her luminescent veil.
Caught in her satiny web,
I open my arms
And we both lift night cups
And call a toast to the deep, soft sky,
To the plants all breathing there in the dark,
The moths fumbling the door with their sandy wings,
To the frogs cranking it up down in the marsh
And the smell of rose knifing in on a breeze.

We call a toast to a night in High Summer
And we drink and drink and drink
In celebration.

Return

After the cutting and the poisons
I take my old dog, who is blind,
Onto the path winding beside the choke cherry and brambles,
The milkweed that bobble their soft, purple flower heads in a small breeze.
We pass beside the creek
Where the black willow stretches out her limbs along the bank
And tosses her hair into the water eddies,
The marsh, where frogs slush into the water at our footsteps,
And the red winged blackbird poses on a high stalk
To fan its brilliant stripe for us.

We step out onto the field that flows away in waves of grasses
To be held by a ring of blue mountains.
The field, where we have watched and smelled and heard and touched
All the seasons dance and turn
And turn again.
We climb the first small rise
And, among the sentinels of the orange broom sage,
We lie down.
And my old dog places his muzzle in my palm.

The sky and the clouds of the day pass over us
And the shadows of the trees at the field's edge flow across us.
Still we lie there.
The evening swallows stitch the air above us
And the smell of dark gathers.
Still we lie there.
We lie in the field until something ineffable
Passes from the skin of the earth into my skin
And then we rise,
And without stumbling,
Find our way home.

[Published in **Artemis** XXII 2015]

Two by Two

Liberation
Juice
Eyeball
My Lover
Happy Valentine
Tea

liberation

in the tobacco barn
I sort stalks all night
itching   sand up to my ankles
your blue truck roars
in at midnight
you bring fox babies
their paws dark and shapely
eyes little black seeds
stuck in red fur
I dig a burrow in the yellow sand
and roll them in

after a kiss
a listless squeeze
you blaze away
back to the spoiled wife and kids
the house on the hill
choices you made long ago

at dawn
three men come for you
they squat and poke
cracked fingers into the sand
they tell me you have
let the foxes loose again
they tell of coming
around a bend at dusk
and seeing the foxes trotting behind you
away from the cages
that line their farm
their eyes are flat
and blue as chicory
run over on a road bed

I remember turning
to you on a bed
with a stained canopy
I think of you rising
from the streaming creek
the hairs on your body
pressed down flat and slick

I give them
the little foxes
they are light as I lift them
their eyes wet and rimmed
with sand grains   they pant
as they leave me

I press my hands
to my face and smell
tobacco and wild fur

*[Published in the **Sun**, Jan. 2002: Issue 313]*

Juice

I arrange a lush fruit bowl
of words
composing the poem as carefully
as I might lean deep orange moons
of sliced papaya   against
yellow slips of mango   stack wet red
watermelon pyramids
beside slick pineapple rounds

my last offering
to tempt his soul's appetite

surely here, where the tropical air
runs its tongue   inside our clothes
and pink bougainvillea curves taffeta blossoms
over our netted doorway

surely here   this folded man will open
will sing the song behind his   greedy consumption
of my body each night
after which he turns away   flinching
if I seek comfort or words

in this place where   jungle lily
sends out her dark perfume
and hidden birds call through the canopy
where the frog sings poing poing   as night falls
surely here
he will assuage my fears

I offer the poem at our bamboo table
under wide spinning fans
after breakfast dishes are cleared
he reads   his eyes hooded
his face flat and cool as the square tiles
beneath our feet

this word   he says
tapping his groomed forefinger on the page
this word should never be hyphenated he flicks
the poem into the circle of water
left by his glass.

his chair scrapes delicately   his napkin
goes beside his plate
he saunters across the veranda
no backward glance

the paper lies open
on the table   one corner lifting
in the sultry breeze
the ink blurs and runs into a bruised oval
like a guava   giving up its juice
like a wound

Eyeball

you came to town
in a traveling troupe
of Bulgarian dancers
during the matinee
your glass eye winked
at me in the second row

instead of dinner
I took you to my studio
you danced evil
your eyeball was presumptuous
your eyeball spoke in rhyme
your eyeball clicked time
socket socket socket bone

I photographed you
until all my film was gone
I told you the story of Sweet William
star of fourth grade
washing his eye in the water fountain
at recess

one day he rolled it
down my palm
it was hard bright blue
complete with tiny red forked veins
that night I dreamed
Sweet William took out his eye
rolled it round my body
till it glittered
seeing things in me
no one had ever seen before

you said come to Bulgaria
we will breakfast on honey bread
and clotted cream
you will have my eye served in a tiny eggcup
once a day

we said goodbye
to the sound of balalaikas
socket socket socket bone

*[Published in **Artemis** VII 1984]*

My Lover

has creased my neck with his stiletto mustache
    lifted   the hairs on my body
with his secrets

leaving me wet starving
he closes me out of the shower
and one by one   presses body parts
onto the glass door
    for me to see
pearl string of the spine   slit
    tumor of the lips
forearm like the underbelly
    of some lank fish
blind phallas   slipping
    on the soapy glass

it is only his fingertips
    flat fleshy tidbits
spun in ancient whorls
that tell me   what I know
and do not know
    of him

*[Published in **Rip Rap** 41 2018]*

Happy Valentine

The venison medallions
Simmer in the sauce
Like three lopsided valentines
On this cold February fourteenth.

After spitting at each other in the van
Like angry cats,
What else can I offer
Than this body food?

I have already given you
The true gift of my anger,
Often held back, hidden
To implode and burn us a future time.

Today it was given freely,
Raw as blood,
Red and perfect
As a heart.

Tea

Curtains closed against the night
But the porch light burns
In competition with the half-moon
Strung in bare branches.
The smell of mildew on the stoop.
Clean Zen emptiness inside.
Do I smell contentment
Or loneliness?
I have forgotten your tallness,
How I have to look up.
Still handsome, slender, silver hair your only aging.
You are wearing silly child's slippers with cuffed tops,
Innocent to their appeal.
Your innocence always so much a part of your charm.

We do not hug.
I ask for tea
Your familiar hands present the Tazo choices-
Passion or *Calm*
You make a joke about my choice of *Calm*
And toss the square, purple packet of *Passion*
Back onto the counter, unopened.

≫≪

Spirit

Communion Sunday
Love With The Moon Priestess
Poem to Mary's Eggs
Between the Hair and the Celestial Heart
to one of the homeless in our capitol
startlingly blue sanpaku
House Sitting for the Shaman
Choosing
to the full moon
Dreams

Communion Sunday

The Church is old
edged by a marsh
the pews grow tiny doors
that open and close with a noise
like wings   you are

beside me   heavy and reluctant
in serge   this morning
we visited the traps   the marsh
stank of sea fog and spoor   among the soft
muskrat mounds   your boxes squat

there is only one muskrat
his spine locked   his body tumescent
in the final paroxysm   you bend close to him
your beard touches his fur   you croon

"musquash musquash"   and finger
the shape of his skull   now
the marsh laps on the church stoop
the altar seeps   you drag me
forward   the wafer cleaves
to your tongue.

*[Published in **Jam Today**]*

Love With The Moon Priestess

cupping both hands
I offer You a geode
thunderegg cleft open
gelatinous sparkle   sweet
jellyroll
inside the egg juice   pink
the color of the chakra for peace
You dip in your fingers   smear
glitter in a thin glaze
        over the third eye
the Horned God snorts
among the silver maples
seeds scatter like diamonds
        across the fields
with stars baying   You lean close
and whisper
the secret   lays me open
        delicate fillet
between bone and heart   yearning
until the moon turns me inside out
        until I swarm her   in a web
with other stars

Poem to Mary's Eggs

This morning
Two orange suns in the black cast iron sky pan.
Mary's eggs told me   flat out
That I was a divine being
My soul close to the edges of my body
Dancing a karma I would never understand   so give it up.
I cried   and laughed
And gobbled them up salty
And us three
Are one.

Between the Hair and the Celestial Heart

(for Katy)

saying goodby
I slip into your embrace
                and find myself
between the hair and the celestial heart
between earth   and heaven
your hair
a river of silk   falling over my arms
smelling of deep forest and light
your cheek   the shape I have always known
our hearts coiling open   ripe with the bliss of stars
why is it   with some people   we feel what we all long for?
we feel the oneness   palpable
     waiting
         infinite

to one of the homeless in our capital

with the blanket draped over your shoulders
barely sweeping the tips of new grass
you seem to levitate as you glide towards us
the patina of grime on your skin
turning bronze-flecked in the late afternoon sun

behind you the washington monument rises
pure and lofty as a temple

my small daughter and I stand transfixed as you bear down on us
the nimbus of your deranged hair flaring softly
your nails gleaming
you stretch out your hand as if in absolution
your amber eyes looking into us as if you know everything
everything
as if you see our souls floating like smoke
upon our bones

startlingly blue sanpaku

(a twister for forked tongues for bob from
gertrude, the snake)

summon me to winter debris nest
call me gertrude   trickster   I enjoy
your gifts   words flat skipping stones
telling a life   startlingly blue
sanpaku eyes

this woman would heal   gently
take the nape of the neck   open
the vertebrae   let shadows
spill out onto the palms
you would   empower
enter the solar plexus   shape
manifestations with smoking fingers

i would coil eternity
fix your place in the stars
remind you   you must truly shed
your skins

let the fear of my metallic eye
strike into the marrow of the bone
(for I am more than what I seem)
let the shyness of this spring day
flood the oasis of the soul
(for it nourishes that which is concealed)
let the softness of gosling down
caress the ancient spiral of fingertips
(for that is where the spirit dances)

never forgetting the power absolute

the dogtooth violet   splitting
unnoticed   through the rock

[Published in *Artemis XII* 1989]

House Sitting for the Shaman

Knowledge spins in these ancient stones
seeping into my dreams   bobcat and coon
bones   struggle and death
loneliness and the cries of animals
outside   Sugar Loaf Mountain rears against the sky
like a giant tsunami   poised
to cast a spell of waiting

I learn rhythms
when the wasps sleep
what hour the stained glass suffuses with color
when deer amble the lawn

          An after-image   the shaman lingers in the shadows
brown forearms thrusting from gauzy sleeves
bristle of mustache
mask cracked open
multi-colored hair crawling from collar toward throat

I trace the spoor of him
hunting power
slide on his work gloves to heft the hand scythe
                                        study the swirl of his
shaving brush
find his pink flamingo shorts at frolic on the floor
there are no secrets
and I am restless in the shaman's bed
finding no scent   no body imprint
in which to settle my own bones

Choosing

I feel them handle me   gently unwrap
the swaddling   tend
the bites of the dark man on throat
and shoulders

when my eyes open
I sit propped in the prow
of a low-slung skiff sliding
through black waters   soft mist settling
like a cloak

I look back to where they perch   squabbling
quietly about our destination
Jesus the Buddha and the Goddess   toeing
one another for room

Jesus' bloody heart   winks
like red neon
in his cellophane chest   all
the Buddha's words
sound like the mighty OM

but oh   the Goddess
her thighs rear like trees
her eyes reflect   the indigo
of the night sky   all
the fishes and animals of the wilds
shimmer in the weaving of her dress
bees   cluster
her breasts
for honey suck
in the dark cavern of her womb   the walls weep
mother's tears
and blind things move in the deep
underground springs

I beckon her forward
her arms come around me
like mountains   like rivers
we put our heads together for   girl
talk   and whisper

her words prickle   with the shine and glitter
of moonlight   her long tangled
hair smells of the sea

once chosen
she stands   and commands
the mist
with a sweep of her arms
there on the far bank
the Summer Country   unfurls
its sunlit beauty   the sounds of celebration
call us forward
the murmur of voices   the laden table
beneath the trees.

to the full moon

out howling in this burning light   every egg
straining to burst its nimbus and be sucked back
oh   this clutch of astral orbs
glimmering like serpent spawn and mistletoe

we we are inchoate
the rich entelechy of our forms
opening and closing to your rhythm
the light   sparking
from out the vegg
streaking across the land
like the faerie arms of succubus
awaiting exaltation / annihilation
the long sigh of giving up   up
up to press flesh with the flesh of the moon

[Published in Artemis XXVII 2020]

Dreams

Egypt, and my bed is full of dreams,

So vibrant they breathe and sparkle in my hands
With hues so deep they saturate my eyes.
And I wake with life's mysteries revealed,
Or drawn into a deeper mystery.

Does the light desert air conjure a mirage
To tremble on the edges of my sleep,
The fragrant visions coming swiftly
With no damp particles to stay their flight?

Maybe specters ride the droning waver of the call to prayer
That floats from the curved minarets rising like wraiths
From the Cairo skyline.

Or when these wrapped and bandaged women
At night uncoil the shawl and mask,
Do their sumptuous imaginings drop like jewels from unbound hair
And, sighing, find their way into my sleep?

Or perhaps in the deepest tenor of the night
The pyramids themselves begin to stir
Their four-sided peaks rending the sky
And the old Pharaonic Gods wake in that land alight with fancy,
Where the temple priestess was taught to roam
Far from her body gathering wisdom during sleep.

While I slumber, does Anubis draw back lips from canine teeth,
And breathe his secrets in my ears,
And the eye of Horus stare me like the moon?
Does Isis kneel above me with fluted wings outspread,
Her dappled lion curled about her knees,
Lotus perfume dropping from her hair,
Her feathers reaching
Stirring the veil between the worlds?

꒰ꕤ꒱

Poems for Children

My Giddylout
John's Mountain
Ballyhoo
Dragon candy
Plishy Plashy
Golden Fellow
Bee Song
Nap Time
Apple rhyme
Nest

My Giddylout

My Giddylout
Is thin for a lout.
She doesn't stand around,
She whirls about.
She has a crystal nose
And a purple thumb
And whenever I whistle
She always comes.
She comes whizzing like a gizmo
Or rolling like a ball.
She never walks straight,
She never stands tall.
She wears a silver feather
And a gown that's red
And a hat that spins
Round and round on her head.

She takes me wherever
I want to go.
We always zip along.
We never go slow.
We might go slipping
Underneath the ground,
Scare the moles in their holes
And whisk through gopher town.
We might go spinning
Up to the stars
To kiss the moon's face
And streak past Mars.

We might come to visit you
But you'll never know.
We'll be whizzing oh so fast
And you'll be moving slow.
But if you feel a breeze
When there's no breeze about
Or hear someone shouting
When there's no one to shout
Or see a falling star
When no stars are out -
Just remember what I told you
About my Giddylout.

John's Mountain

John was beginning
To be an old man.
He wanted to turn himself
Into a piece of land.
He stuck up his knees
And called them each a mountain.
He pulled the hairs out of his head
And started into counting –
Twenty-six, twenty-seven,
Twenty-eight, twenty-nine-
He set them on his knees
And called them Jack Pines.

He made a rocky knob
Out of his nose.
He made river pebbles
Out of each of his toes.
His eyes were two lakes,
Wet and blue and round.
His mouth was a cavern
Going far underground.
He made a bushy thicket
Out of his beard
And deep sinkholes
Out of each of his ears.

His chest was a valley.
His stomach was a hill.
He laid down twenty years ago.
He's lying there still.
You can stand on the top
Of John's Mountain gap
And look down at John
Lying out like a map.

Ballyhoo

What can you do
With a Ballyhoo?
If you don't like it
Mash it with your shoe.
If you like it
Wear it on your head.
If you love it
Tuck it into bed.
Wake it early.
Feed it from your plate.
Send it out to play,
Let it stay out late.
Prance with it, prance with it,
Do a little dance with it,
Learn to take a chance with it,
Wear a pair of pants with it.
What can you do
With a Ballyhoo?
I know some things -
Now how about you?

Dragon candy

Dragon candy slides and slips
Slithers down between your lips.
Sounds like *hissss* and *frang* and *groat*,
Builds a fire in your throat.
Dragon toenails, dragon scales,
Tiny lashings of a tail.
Smoke comes dancing out your nose,
In your eye the sun just rose
Bright and hot and dandy, dandy
Just like dragon candy.

Plishy Plashy

Plishy plashy moths on dresses
Swif it on the by
whisper wings
and bunny brushes
shipping in the sky
shake out dust out
rags and snags and roundabout
see what I found out about
mothy dothy pie.

Golden Fellow

There was a golden fellow
Came down from the sun.
He said he'd like to tell me
Everything I've done.
He said he's been watching me
Every single day
But I grew afraid
And ran away.

Bee Song

A truck full of bees
Stung me on the knees.
Out from the stings
Sprouted red clover.
It kept on sprouting
Till I'd sprouted all over.
Come back bees
Come back and suck.
Take full bellies
Home in your truck.

Nap Time

When nap time comes
And I lie down to sleep
Sometimes I feel fingers
Tickling my feet.
Sometimes I feel feathers
Tipping my nose,
Wiggly wiggly wormies
Cawling 'round my toes.
Something awful fuzzy
Curls up behind my knees.
Something buzzes in my ears.
I think it's honeybees.
Something dances, prances
All around my chest
And I try and I try
But I just can't rest.

Apple rhyme

Apple rhyme, apple rhyme,
Try to paint a squiggly line
Joying curvy tops and tips,
Cherry, curry, cherry lips
Kiss it on the apple rhyme,
Sip a rust red sip of time.
Sipper of the whistle train
Seek the apple branch again,
Spit the smoke and cinder must,
Sup upon the apple dust.
Apple rhyme, apple rhyme
Shiny, curvy slips of time
Push it into blossom line
Slide it down the apple rhyme.

Nest

I have a brown bird
that lives in my hair
she feeds on the sweet peas
growing there
and when the sun
has left the day
I send her out
to find her prey.
She brings me reeds
and tamarind fish
and we eat them
off a silver dish.

One day she flew out
and didn't come back.
I called her till
the day grew black.
She came flying home
by the light of the moon,
carrying a horn
and a silver cocoon.
The horn went on my head
and I wore it like a hat.
The cocoon opened up
and out came a bat.
It tickles my eyelids
and licks up my tears
and hangs upside down
from one of my ears.

୨୦⊷

Senator

Mama always told me I could gentle things, wild things, nervous things, scared things. We had a sow that ate her piglets and I knew it was just because she was scared of the sound of our mule wagon rolling down the rutted road beside the pig lot just minutes after her piglets were born. She grew more nervous after that and would try to attack Daddy when he came with a pail of slops. But I could ease myself into the lot and scratch her back with a corncob till she quieted and she never bothered me.

Two summers ago, when I was only a girl of ten, I tamed a baby flying squirrel that I found with a broken leg under one of our big oak trees in the grove. I kept him in a shoebox with an old towel, fed him warm milk out of an eyedropper and then gave him bits of fruit and seeds. He would sit on my shoulder and when people came near he would make his way down into my apron pocket and poke his sleek head out to look at them, but he wouldn't let anyone touch him but me. When his leg healed, Mama made me put him back in the grove late one evening just as the sun went down. I thought he would still be there in the morning, waiting for me, but I never saw him again. When I complained to Mama she gave me a swift hug. "The wild takes care of the wild." She said.

The truth is, I love the wild in things. It calls me and I want to get up next to it, smell the fear, feel the thrill. I think that's what I loved about Senator. He was the black stallion stud that Daddy thought was going to be our way out of debt.

It took four men to unload Senator from the truck. He was rearing and charging; lifted little Jimmy Deal clear off the ground, his hooves so black they looked dipped in ink, his mane and tail snapping in the air. The scent of wild came off him like smoke.

The next day I woke up to hear him crashing around in his stall, the sound coming muffled in through the open window. I eased out from beside my eight-year-old sister who was never an early riser.

Light was staining the eastern sky but the sun wasn't yet up. I slipped into my blue day dress and apron, took the lantern and went down into the root cellar to get three apples. The dew wet my brown farm boots as I passed under the wide maple, down past the chicken house to the barn. As I got close, the noise stopped and I knew the stallion was listening to my approach. I cracked the tall door open. The barn was full of the smell of horse and fear, a rank smell, so thick and alive it was like a wall. As I walked into it toward his stall, Senator called and lunged forward striking his hooves on top of the gate. I lifted up the lantern and he backed away to the far corner. His eyes rolled white and he pumped his massive neck up and down. I came steady on watching him and began to sing a short children's song under my breath. "Sing a song of sixpence, pocketful of rye...4 and twenty blackbirds baked in a pie..." I placed the three apples on the top of the stall's gate and slowly sauntered back to the barn door. At the door I turned and at that moment the sun came slanting in, lighting up the motes of dust raised by Senator's hooves. He and I surveyed each other through a haze of floating debris. He made no move toward the apples, but when I came back to the barn after I had gathered the eggs from the henhouse, they were gone and it seemed to me he had a calmer look in his eyes. He backed into the corner of his stall again and we looked at one another, his large black eyes staring into my blue ones. But I quickly shifted my gaze, as I knew to never stare into a male animal's eyes for long because they may take it as a challenge.

During the next weeks, I watched them work Senator in the makeshift ring and gallop that Daddy had put up in the lower field. He had hired Jackson Barlow, a local man reported to "have a way" with horses. The Barlow brothers also had a reputation for bad tempers and drinking and I had heard Mama tell Daddy she didn't like having him about the farm. Daddy replied that Barlow was his best bet in getting Senator calmed down enough to hold at stud and didn't she want a new source of income coming in? Jackson Barlow was a short, wiry man with small, mean eyes. His way with horses seemed harsh to me. Every day he worked the horse until Senator was ragged. Using a long, wicked whip to keep him going, he lunged the horse around and around the ring. Senator's head was bowed down when he returned to his stall, his sides slick with sweat and sometimes blood. But Jimmy Deal still had to clip him into two head chains to wash him down because once Senator swung his great body and tried to crush Jimmy against the side of the barn.

I kept my early morning trips to the barn. I kept singing the blackbird song and the apples always disappeared. The middle of the second week I started to stay to see if Senator would let me watch him claim his early morning treats. The first time, still singing, I stopped and leaned in the barn door in the half-light, occasionally flickering my glance toward the horse. He blew out his nostrils at me and pumped his head. Then very slowly he came forward and with the most delicate of gestures, swung up his large head, puckered the wide lips and plucked the apples, one by one, to crunch and swallow. Each morning after that I moved a little closer. The fifth morning I left my hand beside the apples on top of the gate. Senator snorted and pawed the air, but then quickly sucked up the treats and retreated to the back of his stall, his eyes never leaving me. I left my hand on the stall for three more days and the forth day I balanced one of my apples on my palm on top of the gate. "Sing a song of sixpence..." I began, barely above a whisper. I kept singing as the horse paced in the back of his stall, rolling his eyes in my direction, giving little hops when he turned. After I finished the song, I turned and left, taking all the apples with me, not looking back. The next morning I set them out again with the third one again in my palm. Senator watched, he shook his head so hard strings of slobber flew from his lips. He turned and made a small rearing motion, his sharp front hooves rising about two feet from the barn floor. Then he slowly approached. My body tensed. Part of me wanted to snatch my hand away, worried he would bite or nip to get his treat, but the other part of me felt that thrill to be so connected to something so big, so alive, so wild. I kept singing and closed my eyes. I laid my palm as flat as I could against the top of the gate without dropping the apple. After a moment I heard the dull thud of his hooves moving closer. The deep, tangy smell of horse enveloped me, then the sound of his breath and the warm stream of it on my fingers. And finally the soft, prickly- haired muzzle and the muscular lips working to capture the apple with no harm to my hand. The apple gone, I opened my eyes. The stallion stayed there, his head next to mine. He crunched his treat and I slowly pulled back my arm. Again we regarded each other. I did not move away and he did not retreat. Did something pass between us at that moment? I like to believe it did. I believe he began to see me as someone he could trust, someone on his side, someone he could look at eyeball to eyeball, without challenge.

When I entered the barn the next morning Senator thrust his large head over the gate and whickered as though he were calling in his treats. From then on he ate directly from my palm. I added carrots to the apples and began to steal the square, grainy lumps of sugar from the blue bowl on the kitchen table. Mama almost caught me once, coming into the kitchen as I was pocketing the sugar lumps. I tilted the egg-gathering basket on my arm so she couldn't see the carrots resting in the bottom. She praised my industriousness and gave me a little pat on the shoulder as I moved away from her.

I began to pet Senator, gingerly at first, moving my hand up over the side of his jaw after he had plucked the treats from my hand. When he didn't seem to mind, I would run my hand down the side of his thick black neck, reach underneath and pat it from the other side. I ran my hand through his coarse mane and combed his forelock between his ears with my fingers. Sometimes he would move away, but often he stayed where he was and once he dropped his head down over the stall door and pressed the front of his head into the front of my chest. I was so surprised I almost jumped, but forced myself to be still and hold my breath, hoping the moment would last. He nudged at me with his great head on one side and then the other and I realized he was sniffing for more sugar where I carried it in my apron pockets. From then on that became a game for us. I would give him one lump of sugar from my hand and leave two lumps in my pockets, sometimes in the right pocket, sometimes in the left. When he found the right pocket and gave it a sharp nudge, I would withdraw the sugar and he would take it from my palm.

We had our rituals, he and I. Every time I came into the barn I sang the blackbird song. Then after the apples and carrots, the sugar lumps. Then the petting and sometimes he would put his soft nose alongside my head and blow his warm breath through my hair. And we would look at one another, eyeball to eyeball.

I had stopped going to the ring where Jackson Barlow worked Senator because I couldn't stand to see the way the man seemed to enjoy punishing the horse, lunging him around and around the ring with no breaks for water, cracking him with the tip of the whip when he faltered. When I complained to Daddy he said Barlow knew what he was doing, but I heard Jimmy Deal tell Daddy that Senator seemed to be getting worse instead of better and that twice Barlow had showed up drunk and Jimmy had sent him home.

The next day I was down in the garden picking potato bugs off the vines when I heard Senator scream from the ring. I had never heard a noise like that noise. It sounded almost human. It tore me open and I threw down my bucket and ran.

Jackson Barlow and Senator both lay in the dirt. Daddy was on his knees beside Barlow and Senator was on his side with one foreleg folded up in a crooked angle. Jimmy Deal was sitting on his heaving neck so he couldn't get to his feet. Senator was thrusting out his back legs and screaming but Jimmy hung on. I climbed the fence in one swift move and ran to Senator. When he saw me he stopped struggling and lay his massive neck down into the dirt. I knelt beside his head and he quieted; his breath heaved and his eyes cleaved to mine. A pool of saliva gathered under his open mouth. Someone began shouting behind me and I turned to see Barlow sitting up, cursing a blue streak at Daddy. Then I saw Daddy draw back his fist and cuff Barlow back to the ground. I had never seen Daddy do anything like that, and when he told me to run quick back to the house and stay there, I flew.

Mama wouldn't let me go back to the ring, so I went to the barn. His smell was still there, soaked into the wood, the straw, the air. I ran my hand along the top of the stall door where I had first set the apples. I couldn't cry because a dryness was in me, like all the water in the world wouldn't fill me enough to make tears. But I could sing and I sang the blackbird song. Then the shots came – one and then two. I don't even like to imagine why it took two. Maybe they had to kill his body, then kill the wild in him: maybe the wild just wouldn't die. I thought of what Mama had said – "The wild takes care of the wild." But I couldn't make my mind understand it. And I felt old, older than twelve. I felt like I might never understand anything again.

*[Published in **Floyd County Moonshine: Ten Year Anniversary Special Edition:** Issue 10.1-2 Fall 2018]*

‍‍

John Epps and Miss Bessie

John Epps, a thin, balding man of forty-eight, turned into Cobb's Drugstore at the corner of First and Market. He went right past the newspapers proclaiming "I like Ike!" and walked straight to the counter containing cough syrups, nose drops and other cold remedies. As he picked up his weekly supply of cough drops, which he sucked daily to prevent getting a cough, a large poster above the counter caught his attention. On the left side of the poster was the profile of a man with his mouth open. Out of his mouth and spreading across the right side of the poster were millions of tiny gray and green dots. The caption read, "One Sneeze Can Cause Millions of Tiny Germs." John Epps drew in his breath and blinked his pale blue eyes. "So that's what they look like." He whispered. As if in answer, the small dots drifted off the poster and formed a gray and green cloud around his head.

John Epps ran, screaming, from the drugstore. He didn't scream again until he was five blocks down and two stories up, behind the slammed door of his bachelor apartment. This time it was a short squeak of relief. The cloud was gone.

John Epps wiped the sweat from his forehead with his fingertips and looked slowly around the apartment. He closed all the windows. He folded a clean white towel and pressed it into the crack under the door, then lit a roll of newspaper and passed the flame slowly over all of his appliances and furniture. The clothes he was wearing he took off and dropped into a large pot of boiling water. At twelve-thirty, after a scalding shower, he crawled under his covers and fell into a deep sleep.

John Epps dreamed of his mother, who turned into a very large, very dirty frog. He was chasing her with a bottle of red rubbing alcohol that shone like a light, when suddenly his eyes jerked open. Covering his bedspread in a gray and green film, climbing in rings up the furniture, dripping in through the cracks in the windows, teeming underneath his fingernails, were the germs.

———————

Ever since she had been sixteen, Miss Bessie had creamed her face with Dr. Ox Skin Cream for an hour every night. Her skin looked like the skin of a pearl. It was the only beautiful thing about her. She was John Epp's third cousin. She was eleven years older then he was. Once, when she was fourteen and all the relatives had come for Christmas, she had secretly pulled John underneath the mistletoe and pressed his wet baby's mouth to hers. Then she had run into the bedroom and cried. It was the only kiss she had ever had.

Until her father had died and left her a "considerable sum," Miss Bessie had run a boarding house outside a small mountain town in southwest Virginia. Now Bessie's rooms were closed and she lived there alone. She was not really lonely. She had five cats.

Miss Bessie laid the letter flat on the dresser and read it again while she creamed her face. It was from John Epp's sister. It said that John had been in the state hospital and that he wanted to come to the country for a rest and would she open a room for him. It said he had some peculiar habits. It said everything must be very clean. That part made Bessie a little angry. It made her remember John's mother. Whenever they had come to visit, John's mother had washed her hands a lot and kept a pot of water boiling on the stove to "sterilize" things. Miss Bessie hadn't seen John or his family since they moved up north to Philadelphia twenty years ago. She had written back and said yes, she would open a room for him.

At ten fifteen Saturday morning, Howie Bradshaw's truck stopped in front of her house. He had brought John up from the station. Miss Bessie took off her apron, ran her stubby fingers over her hair and went quickly to the dining room window. John Epps wore a black suit and a black hat. He was very thin and his nose was very beaked. He reminded Miss Bessie of a marsh bird. A bittern. Coming up the walk, he held his arms a little bit up in the air at an angle away from his body. He let Howie carry all the luggage.

Miss Bessie stepped out onto the porch. "Mornin' Howie. Hello John. It's been a long time." John Epps jumped slightly when he heard his name. Miss Bessie held out her hand. John Epps didn't move, but stared at her outstretched palm. His gaze ran slowly up her arm, across her bosom to her face and back down to her feet. Finally he grasped her hand and quickly let go.

At his look, Miss Bessie's translucent skin had turned pink. She felt as though someone had pressed a hot wash cloth to her chest. "Howie, take John's things to the downstairs room," she said in a queer voice.

John Epps peered anxiously around his room. Everything was clean. Everything was very clean. Miss Bessie stood with her hands pressed together in the doorway. "Is everything all right, John?"

"Yes, yes, It's very clean."

"The bathroom is right down..."

"No!"

"No?"

"I mean...I don't.... There's a spring here, isn't there?"

"Why yes, right down in the edge of the woods." She was surprised he remembered.

"Will you...can you walk down there with me and show me?"

"Now?" Miss Bessie's heart began to beat fast.

"Yes...if you don't mind?"

"Oh yes, yes. Just let me...I'll only be a minute." Miss Bessie went quickly to her room. She looked anxiously at her face in the mirror. It was the same - heavy jaw, bulbous nose, eyes that almost crossed. From the top of her closet, Miss Bessie took down a hat. It was a cream-colored straw with a lime scarf that went around the crown and came down through two holes to tie under her chin. She put on a lime green sweater and folded two clean handkerchiefs into the pocket of her white dress.

John Epps was on the porch. He had taken off his coat and was in his shirtsleeves. A gold watch chain glittered against his black vest. "You don't mind? I didn't mean to..." He slid his hands rapidly in and out of his pockets.

Miss Bessie flushed, "Oh no, no. Why it's a beautiful day for...a walk."

John Epps looked around him as though for the first time. He took a long breath and his shoulders relaxed. He smiled at Miss Bessie. "Yes, yes it is. It is beautiful."

They took the path that went down through two fields in back of the house. When they came to the old-fashioned stile that spanned the fence, John went over first and stood to one side. He offered Miss Bessie the back of his hand with a courtly gesture as though leading her out onto the dance floor. Her hand lingered upon his like the moth lingers near the flame.

It was early spring, and on their left, Brush Mountain loomed up in a haze of pale green sprinkled with pink. Nestled in the corner of the field, the plum thicket was in bloom. Thin black branches thrust sharply up into a shimmering mass of petals. As they passed, some of the small white blossoms drifted down against John Epp's black vest and onto the brim of Miss Bessie's hat. Deep in the thicket, a bird called out a strange, wild note. Miss Bessie felt as if that bird were in her very own breast.

Going down the creek that day, they had found three springs. John Epps visited them daily. The first he drank from. The second he washed his face in. In the third he washed the rest of his body. His clothes, Miss Bessie boiled twice a week. His breakfast was always pancakes. "Flapjacks" he called them. First, Miss Bessie would make a huge flapjack the size of the pan. He would take it, right up from the pan still steaming hot, and run it all over the face of his plate. Then he would wipe his knife and fork with it. Then Miss Bessie would take it outside for her cats. Her cats had been house cats for ten years. Now they were back porch cats. Then John Epps would eat five smaller flapjacks with fresh butter and sorghum. His lunch was always boiled, his dinner baked. He did not eat meat.

Every evening after supper, John Epps and Miss Bessie would take a walk. Miss Bessie would walk close to him and watch his long, fine hands flash in the gathering dark as he told her about his afternoons down at the post office. It was a gathering place for the rural neighborhood. There were straight back chairs set all around the lobby and they were always filled. He loved to listen to stories of coon hunts in the dead of night, and who caught the biggest fish and who was getting married or having a baby. It all seemed so simple to him, so clean and unconfusing. He had almost forgotten his life in the city. And he liked to come home and eat supper and walk with Miss Bessie. He would walk close to her and listen to the rustling of her spotless dress with the clean scent of starch coming from it.

One day in early autumn, John Epps pushed back his chair from lunch and laid his napkin carefully beside his plate. Miss Bessie was at the stove bending over a pot of boiling clothes.

John cleared his throat. "Bessie?"

"Yes, John?"

"Howie had a little talk with me down at the post office yesterday."

"He did?"

"Yes...he said you and I were being talked about."

Miss Bessie turned to him. Her face was red from the steam. "Talked about?"

"Yes, he told me people are talking."

"I don't understand John. Talking about what?" Miss Bessie's eyes were round.

John Epps looked at the floor. "He said...well...about the fact that we're living here...alone."

Miss Bessie's heart gave a funny little jump. She bent over the pot again.

"Howie says people say I should leave..." Miss Bessie stood still. She couldn't speak. "...or that we should get married."

Silence.

"That would make things more...convenient. Wouldn't it Bessie? ...Bessie?"

Miss Bessie turned around. Her face was like a piece of the sun. "Yes John," she whispered. "Yes, anything you want."

After John left for the post office, Miss Bessie held up her apron and did a little dance in the middle of the floor. Then she cried awhile. Then she went all over the house and flung back the curtains in every room. She even went into old boarders' rooms she never used.

She decided to make a cake. Spice cake with caramel icing was John's favorite. Taking out molasses and milk, she knocked the two together and the milk spilled into a big pool on the floor. The molasses splashed in big drops onto her bosom. Miss Bessie laughed. She wiped a drop off with her finger and popped that finger in her mouth.

She opened the back door and called her cats, "Kitty-kitty, kitty-kitty. Come in for some milk, dears." As they came over the threshold, she clasped each one of them to her for a moment. "Oh, dearie dears, oh dearie, dearie dears," she murmured. The cats stood in a circle and lapped. Some flies had followed them in. They buzzed about the molasses on Miss Bessie's dress. Miss Bessie stood still and looked at the sun pouring in. Her mind was spinning. There was so much to do, so much to think about.

Something moved behind her and she turned. It was John. He was staring at the cats lapping up the milk. He stared at the brown drops and cat hairs and flies on Miss Bessie's bosom. Miss Bessie's hands flew to her hair. "Why John, whatever are you doing back here so soon?"

Then he saw them. One was gray and one was green. They were both in one corner of her mouth. They were round and no bigger than the point of a pin. And as Miss Bessie spoke, they began to move.

*[Published in **Artemis**]*

༄

Caboose

Gay Nell and the doberman were both panting; the dog from the stagnant heat that had gathered in the upstairs hall where he lay on guard in front of the closed bedroom door, Gay Nell from the exertion of pulling her eighty-two year old body upright against the pink ruffled pillows at the head of the bed. She closed her blue eyes and rested for a moment, mouth open, wisps of dead-white hair ridged up in tufts around her sweaty forehead. Then she opened her eyes, rolled up the right sleeve of her silky yellow pajamas, bent sideways and fished her fingers into the green glass pitcher of ice water that Billie Gay had left on the bedside table. She pulled out a smooth piece of ice and, with practiced precision, slung out her arm and sent the ice skittering underneath the wide crack at the bottom of the bedroom door. She heard the dog snuffle his nose along the floor, find the ice and slop it up in his jaws. "Bingo! That makes thirty-two." she exclaimed under her breath.

In the last two weeks, thirty-two pieces of ice, hamburger, chicken, egg, and bits of those horrible fish sticks they fed her, all sent under the door to the doberman. If the pieces stuck to the floor, she used the telescoping Grab-It, a device made for old people to reach things on high shelves. It was perfect for extending and pushing the tidbits on under the door. She had asked Billie Gay to leave the Grab-it by her bed in case she wanted to retrieve something from her dresser without getting up.

Billie Gay had found the device and put it in place, all the while picking at her fingernails and hunching thin shoulders, looking out at her grandmother from behind her fringe of dyed black hair with a dazed, sullen look. Gay Nell had decided to try one more time to cut through the fog that surrounded her granddaughter, a fog that almost obscured the Billie Gay that she and Pig had raised.

"Billie Gay," she had made her voice soft and patted the bed beside her. "Darlin', come sit down a minute."

Billie Gay had perched on the edge of the bed, looking down at the floor. Her belly pooched out from between her shiny black cropped top and her low slung black jeans. A belly button ring with a red stone twinkled in the soft, white roll of flesh. An acrid smell came off her clothes.

"Billie Gay, how old are you?"

The girl's head came up, a wary look in her eyes. "You know I'm twenty-three. Why?"

"You and Dwight... Don't you think he's...too old for you?"

Billie Gay had jumped off the bed. "Don't start this talk again, Grandmother!   I know what I'm doing. Dwight and I are...business partners."

Gay Nell kept her voice calm. "What kind of business, Billie Gay?"

Billie Gay had bolted then. "You just don't understand anything!" She slammed the door on the way out. The dog had shifted and growled low in his throat when she flew past him.

Now he was quiet, probably crunching the ice to bits in one bite of his strong jaws. She had seen how powerful they were. Dwight often trained the dog in the back yard where she could see them from her bed. The dog would crouch, then leap and swirl on legs like black springs, his head and neck weaving, biting again and again at the shield covering Dwight's arm. If the window were open she could hear the dog's snarls and the thump of Dwight hitting it down with the shield. He seemed to love taking the dog to the ground, then standing above it, flexing his stringy muscles and cocking his bullet-shaped head up toward her window, his hair buzzed so close Gay Nell could never figure out what color it was. She knew Dwight was trying to wear her down with fear. He didn't understand what a powerful weapon she had —she was old and part of her just didn't care anymore, not about herself anyway. As the young folks said, she "didn't give a shit."

"I don't give a shit!" she hissed at the doberman on the other side of the door. The word "shit" felt good and sharp on her tongue. Somewhere between a secret and a slap. She had never before in her life used language like that. Her mother had told all her daughters, "No one likes to hear ugly words come out of a pretty girl's mouth."   And Pig? Pig would roll in his grave to hear her speak those words. She smiled as she always did when she thought of Pig.

She could see him in her mind, the deep auburn hair springing off his forehead, his barrel chest pushed forward as he strutted on his short legs. More like a bantam rooster, a cock-of-the walk, than a pig. The first year of their marriage her sisters had badgered and badgered her to tell them why she called him Pig, but she never relented. Some things were private, although today it would probably be on reality TV —a whole show on how people got their nicknames.

She recalled the first time she had called him Pig. They had been married four months and he couldn't seem to get enough of her. After they made love he would continue to caress her, smoothing her forehead, rubbing her small hands and feet over and over. He loved to spread her gold hair out on the pillow and push his face through its tousled mass, smelling the lemon verbena she always used as a rinse. One night she spoke sharply because she wanted to get some sleep, "You remind me of a pig rooting around the ground after acorns. Let me go to sleep!"

Delighted, he had thrown back his head and laughed. "A pig, a pig! I'm just a pig at the trough of love!" And he had gathered her in his arms and rolled her around the bed, laughing and repeating the phrase. After that Pig had become the nickname he loved for her to call him. Soon all the family were calling him Pig as easily as though it were his given name.

She twisted in her bed and looked out the window down over the lawn to where Pig had planted a bank of white azaleas under a stand of tall pines years ago. The bend of Shamrock Creek formed a curve there on the border of their ten-acre property. He had worked overtime as a train engineer on the railroad to be able to buy this land and build her this little farmhouse on the prettiest part of the acreage. She and Pig would take a blanket down by the creek in the evenings after supper, lie out and breathe in the spicy, sweet smell of azalea mixed with pine as they watched the creek roll its way down to the Roanoke River.

And now, lying here in their bed, some evenings she saw a light that seemed to glow out from beneath the conifers and she knew it was Pig, down there waiting for her, giving her courage for what she had decided to do. On his deathbed he had squeezed her hands, looked into her eyes and said, "Don't make me wait long." Others said he was delirious from the morphine, but she had known what he meant.

Once, soon after he died, she had shown Billie Gay the glow by the azaleas, told her she thought it was her grandfather. Billie Gay's eyes had filled with tears. "Oh, Mimma, I think it's just the last rays of the sun. I think the diabetes is affecting your eyes." Then Billie Gay had been sorry she had spoken so bluntly and had hugged her grandmother close. "But maybe, Mimma, maybe that's what it is. Maybe it's him." That was when Billie Gay still called her "Mimma" instead of "Grandmother." That was before Dwight had come to live with them and her granddaughter had descended into the fog.

Gay Nell pressed her hands to her chest. A pain ran through her every time she remembered the scene when she discovered what the fog was. It was five months ago, when she could still come and go on the upstairs floor with her walker, before Dwight had given her the doberman as her companion. It was back when Billie Gay still took her downstairs twice a week using the elevator chair that Pig had hired someone to install onto the stair banister when he was diagnosed with heart trouble. She would sit in the chair and it easily ran up and down with a whirring noise, just clearing the steps. She also kept a walker downstairs and she and Billie Gay could even sit on the porch on good weather days.

But all that had changed the night she had gone out in the hall long after they thought she was asleep. She went out because she had begun to hear Billie Gay laughing and talking late at night with Dwight down in the living room. At night she sounded just like her old self, while in the day she seemed solemn and exhausted. Gay Nell was desperate to find out what was happening to her granddaughter.

Gay Nell's walker had wheels so she could come quietly right up to the balustrade of the upstairs balcony that looked down into the living room. Then she had seen them. Billie Gay, half naked, was lying back in Dwight's arms and strewn around them, plain as day, were packets of white powder, a glass pipe and glass vials. All those things, she knew from the TV, were "drug paraphernalia." Dwight looked up and saw her. He leaped up with a curse and took the steps two at a time. He grabbed her and half-dragged her back to her room, pushed her down on the bed and slammed the door on his way out.

She lay there, stunned, and listened as he and Billie Gay had the first of their shouting matches that were now common. She heard him say, "...take that old bitch out!" and "...and get that deed now!"

And Billie Gay was crying and saying, "...my only family!" and "...I won't make her sign..."

Numb, Gay Nell had curled into a ball on the bed and rocked back and forth. All she could think was, Billie Gay and drugs, Billie Gay and drugs! I've lived too long. I've lived too long! Then her mind flew back to when she and Pig took Billie Gay to raise when she was four, after the accident that killed their son and daughter-in-law. Gay Nell had wanted to die then, felt like she was dead, till holding the fragile Billie Gay in her arms and looking down into those hazel eyes just like her son's had brought the life flowing back into her.

Pig had been the strong one then, never seeming to miss a beat. "Courage, my love, that's what life takes," he would tell her as he held her through the long nights. "Let's make the most of what we've got. We've got Billie Gay." Only once had she heard him grieve and that was in the dead of night, when she had wakened and heard a strangled, wailing noise, more animal than human, coming from behind the bathroom door. She had started to go to him but stopped. She knew he would want to keen his dead alone.

Lying there in the fetal position where Dwight had thrown her, she felt too numb to keen, but that's when the plan started forming in her mind. She didn't waste time wondering who was to blame. She knew it was Dwight, knew he was trouble the first time Billie Gay had brought him home. His cold, flat gray eyes, and how he seemed more interested in assessing the house and grounds than in talking to them. Sick as he was then, Pig had known it too. They had tried to talk to Billie Gay, but she hadn't had many boyfriends and was smitten by this thirty-five year old man's attentions. And they didn't want to be too hard on her. She had moved back home to help them with their old-age illnesses.

And now Billie Gay was in his thrall, him and the drugs. Gay Nell had watched the TV, knew if you took certain drugs just one time, you were hooked. But then the plan had started in her mind.

Of course, she hadn't counted on the doberman. Hadn't counted on being held in her room like a prisoner by the black, evil-tempered companion that sprang to his feet, growling, if she even got near the door. Hadn't counted on them taking out her phone, saying they would get her a cell phone soon, that it would be easier for her to use. Not that there was really anyone to call. Her sisters and their husbands all dead, their children scattered across the country, all busy with their own lives. She had been the youngest and now was the last leaf on the tree. She also hadn't counted on Billie Gay giving her a sleeping pill each night, saying it was doctor's orders when she hadn't been to a doctor in months. But the sleeping pills had worked right into the plan.

She reached over to the sweating green pitcher and poured herself a cold glass of water, drank it and settled back into the pillows. This had to be the week the plan was put to work. If she waited much longer, she wouldn't even be able to use the walker. She raised the covers and lifted up her left leg with her hands, pulled up her pajama leg and peeled off the white sock she kept on her foot so she wouldn't have to look at it. Her still-small body made it easy for her to move. Thank goodness she hadn't blown up fat and unwieldy with the diabetes like her older sister. The foot was swollen. It had changed from the bluish purple of last week and was taking on a black hue. The toes looked shriveled at their roots. She had to act soon. At least she was losing feeling in the foot, so it never ached anymore. She pulled the sock back on.

She knew what was happening. The same thing had happened to her sister who had to have both lower legs removed because of gangrene. The problem with Gay Nell's foot had started when she cut her own toe trying to clip her toenails and the cut wouldn't heal. If Dwight had let Billie Gay take her to the doctor, he could have saved her foot. Maybe the doctor still could, after the plan had worked out.

Remember, she told herself, this is nothing compared to Billie Gay being in thrall to that man and the drug. To give herself courage, she turned to the door and spoke loudly, "I don't give a shit!" She heard the doberman get up, roll a growl in his throat, and lie down again.

She let her leg relax down and reached over to the bedside stand to pull out the Bible, King James Version. She knew they would never look there. Opening it to Isaiah 5:11, she counted the sleeping pills laid out in a little row of humps inside the white folded napkin. Twelve, she had been able to hide twelve when they hadn't stood over her to watch her swallow. That should be plenty for the doberman. She had already planned to ask for Beanie-Weenies that day for lunch, knowing she could stick the pills easily inside the little fake hot dog pieces before throwing them under the door.

After lunch, Billie Gay and Dwight always left the house for at least an hour, sometimes two. She thought maybe that they went somewhere to buy or sell drugs. She knew neither of them had regular jobs and Billie Gay was always saying they were business partners. When they came home they would climb upstairs into their bedroom and she would hear the particular squeak made by the hidden panel at the back of their closet. When he built the house, Pig had fixed an extra storage space back there for winter clothes and blankets and had lined it with cedar to keep out the moths. She thought that was where they kept the drugs.

A malodorous smell wafted from under the door and found its way to Gay Nell's nose. The doberman was "letting scents" again. This was a good time to get away from the smell and to take her exercise walk into the bathroom. She closed the Bible, took both hands and waved the book in front of her nose before setting it back on the shelf. "Farting" was what the young people called it now. And it was all over the TV and even in movies. Just like peeing. It seemed like you couldn't watch a week of TV without some man standing at a urinal, talking over his shoulder to someone, while he peed. She wasn't a prude but it just seemed like it would take some of the magic out of a relationship to be constantly exposed to someone's bathroom smells and habits. Thank goodness Pig had agreed with her on that.

But she did miss the TV. Dwight had moved it out of her room last week, telling Billie Gay it was broken, but it wasn't. He was trying to break her down, taking away all of her pleasures. He knew she loved the news and Dr. Phil, and her stories. The characters on "Guiding Light" and "The Days of Our Lives" were like old friends. And all those movies that Billie Gay brought to her, even Dwight's action adventure movies, made her forget, for a little while, the terrible impasse her life had come to. But now, maybe no TV was a good thing. Without it, she could keep her mind focused and sharp.

She pushed herself into a sitting position, threw back the covers and used her hands to put her legs over the side so she was touching the floor with her feet, one sock off and one on. Then she bent forward and dragged the aluminum walker from its place beside the bed. Billie Gay had bought her an expensive kind, with wheels on the front legs and good rubber tips on the back. It even had a little white plastic basket hung between the curved legs so she could carry things about. Using one hand to push, one to pull, she was soon upright and, gripping the walker with both hands, began her slow journey to the master bathroom.

Her left foot was almost completely numb and the material of the white sock kept catching on the floral pattern rug, making her stumble as she swung that leg forward. Holding the walker with one hand, she bent, pulled off the sock and flung it back on the bed. The leg moved easily then and she didn't notice till she was in the bathroom that her foot had completely turned over and she was sliding it along on the fronts of her toes. She dropped herself heavily onto the closed toilet lid, breathing hard.

As she blotted the sweat from her face with a piece of toilet paper, she remembered sitting here a month ago after she had started vacillating, thinking that maybe she was just a crazy old woman for supposing that Billie Gay was in danger. Maybe she hadn't really seen the drugs. Maybe Billie Gay and Dwight just had a—what did they call it on the TV?—a dysfunctional relationship. Maybe Billie Gay was tired of taking care of her and wanted her own life. God knows she herself was tired and just wanted to sink down into old age and rest. If only she could believe all this trouble was just her over-active imagination.

Then she had sat right here on this toilet while Billie Gay was at the grocery store and heard Dwight talking to someone on the phone in the next bedroom. She was sure he thought she was asleep.

"Babe," he had said, "it won't be long now. The old bitch is on her way out and as soon as Billie signs this property over to me, you and I are sittin' on one big piece of change. Developers are crawlin' all over this place... Are you fuckin' kiddin'? I'll get her so strung out she'll sign anything I put in front of her. Then it's you and me, Baby Doll."

She had sat dead still, all breath gone from her chest. So the worst was true. Billie Gay was in harm's way. No matter how old and tired she was, she had to rise up and help her grandchild.

She sat there, waiting for the doberman's scents to subside, enjoying the contrasting light smell of the lemon verbena soap she always asked Billie Gay to put in her bathroom. She knew she had to choose a day for the plan, but whenever she thought of actually carrying it out, a hot feeling of panic rose up and closed her throat, almost making her gag. There were so many things that could go wrong. If just one thing didn't fall into place...

She forced herself to stop her thoughts. Pig always said that too much thinking could drive you crazy. He had told her that when he worked on a big project, like building their house, thinking of the whole thing made it seem impossible. So he made himself think of it as a long stretched-out line. "Like a train, and you just ride one car at a time. Don't even think of the next car. Just ride the one you're on and soon you're at the caboose and the whole thing is done."

She struggled to her feet. She was determined to stop worrying about the whole plan and think of it as a train. So what she could do right now was to check all the train cars, make sure they were all in place and hooked together. She made the few steps to the bathroom window and looked down at the goldfish pond. "Water garden" was what they called it now. Pig had built it the second year they were here, hauling smooth brown rocks from the creek to line the banks. It was beside the brick patio right off the kitchen. When Billie Gay was little she had loved to go out with her grandmother to feed the goldfish after breakfast. She would kneel beside the pond and let the fish food flakes fall slowly from her hand and catch on the surface of the black water between the green disks of lily pad. It thrilled her to see the fish emerge, appearing at first like a smudge of dull orange in the dusky pond, then becoming brighter and brighter till they floated on the surface like golden suns in a dark sky. Billie Gay would work her small mouth in and out of an "O" to mimic their mouths as they gulped the fish food.

The pond had become choked with parrot feather weed after Pig got sick, but Dwight had cleaned it out when he first moved in. Gay Nell had watched him from the window, surprised at the tender way he handled the plants, how he stood back to admire his work as though he were proud. That evening when Billie Gay praised his work to Pig, Dwight had flushed and scowled. Gay Nell turned from the window with a sigh. Goldfish pond—check.

She moved to the small wooden shelf where the old-fashioned oil lamp sat, filled with the fancy, red-colored oil Billie Gay had bought at Walmart. A box of matches lay beside it. Oil lamp—check. Matches— check. She made her way back into the bedroom, noticing her blackened foot was turned over and dragging again. But she seemed to move easier when the foot dragged and there was hardly any feeling left, so she didn't care.

She opened her second dresser drawer and felt underneath her underwear to touch the canceled house insurance policy folded into its envelope. Thank goodness she had refused to give anyone Power of Attorney and Billie Gay had never tried to take over paying the bills. Canceled house insurance policy—check.

From a corner of the drawer she pulled out a piece of paper with a name and phone number. Brendan Dunn. 679-4002. She could see Brendan in her mind's eye when he had come to call on Billie Gay during their last year of high school. He was tall and gawky and shy and once she had seen him draw his hand from behind his back, palming a huge red rose, and offer it to Billie Gay while he kept his eyes on the ground. Billie Gay had been tearful when he and his family moved up north to Boston just a few weeks later. But two years ago Gay Nell had heard he was back in the county, working in the Sheriff's office. And here was that phone number. Pig had made her memorize it in case of emergency. Brendan's number at the Sheriff's office—check.

Tired, Gay Nell rolled to the bed and lay down, quickly stuffing her discolored foot under the covers, out of sight. She eyed the objects on the bedside table. Pen and paper—check. Glass medicine bottle—check. And, of course, sleeping pills in the Bible—check. She pushed the pillows out from under her head so she could lie flat to ease her back.

Her worst worry was the phone. They had taken the phone from her room, but she was sure she had heard its familiar ring coming from the extension in their bedroom, even though they had cell phones. All these gadgets that were supposed to save time just seemed to make things more complicated. She remembered the first phone she and Pig had, a party line, two long rings and a short. She took a deep breath and let it out. Her body began to relax. Remembering the old times, how she and her sisters would chat for hours on the phone, Gay Nell eased into a nap.

When she woke up, it was almost dark and Billie Gay was in her room, pouring water from the green pitcher into the glass. Her face looked puffy and slick, her eyes slitted in the gloomy light. She didn't look at her grandmother. As Gay Nell struggled upright she saw a plate on her bedside stand. The greasy smell of those horrible fish sticks assaulted her nose. The blob of yellowish tartar sauce trailed over the edge of the plate. The heap of store-bought slaw toppled like a tiny wilted haystack.

"Billie Gay," Gay Nell heard her own voice say loudly, "I want Beanie-Weenies for lunch tomorrow."

Billie Gay's eyes flickered over at her with interest, then went dead again. Her voice was a monotone. "Sure, Grandmother, we have plenty of those. Don't forget your sleeping pill." She placed it on the plate beside the fish sticks and left the room. "Stay," she commanded the doberman in a flat tone as she passed him.

Gay Nell fell back on the bed. The die was cast. Try as she might she couldn't keep back the tears. They ran down her cheeks and into her ears and wet the yellow silky collar of her pajamas. Her small sobs sounded like the mewling of a baby. In the midst of it she heard Pig's voice, "Courage, my love, that's what life takes." She straightened up then, dried her tears, and reached for the sleeping pill and water. She would need a good night's rest. She had asked for Beanie-Weenies tomorrow.

She awoke in the late morning out of a dense sleep. Billie Gay had already placed a mini-bagel smeared with cream cheese and a cup of sugared coffee on a tray on the nightstand.

When Gay Nell remembered what the day held, she felt fear drop down over her like a heavy, damp cloak. She lay still and tried to focus her mind. A train... Think of the plan as a train. So...if it's a train, then today is the caboose. Caboose. She had always liked that word. It reminded her of an exclamation point at the end of a sentence. On Fridays she used to pick up Billie Gay from school and they would go down to the railroad yard to watch Pig bring in the four o'clock train. The child loved to see her grandfather sitting at the window of the big engine as it rocked and hissed its way into the station. He would look for them and jauntily tip his striped hat and Billie Gay would laugh with delight. But the thing she loved even more was to watch a train pull out of the yard with the cheery red caboose swaying behind like the happy ending on a long story. Billie Gay would wave both arms and sing, "Little red caboose behind the train, train, train, train!"

Remembering Billie Gay as a child strengthened Gay Nell's resolve. It was almost over. Whatever happened, she would have done her best. Whatever happened, something was bound to change. She sat up and pulled her legs over the side of the bed. "Caboose day!" she said aloud as she grabbed the walker, hefted herself up and made her way to the bathroom, dragging her left foot, for her morning toilet.

It wasn't long after Gay Nell got herself back in bed that Billie Gay came in with a bowl of Beanie-Weenies and a slice of bread. Her hair seemed brittle and her skin gray. A rash of pimples had started up on one side of her chin. As Billie Gay set down the bowl, Gay Nell stretched out her hand. "Billie Gay?"

Her granddaughter stared at the hand then slowly took it in her own. The younger woman's hand was dry and slack, but at its touch, Gay Nell felt her heart turn over in her chest.

She pulled a reluctant Billie Gay one step closer to the bed. "I love you, Billie Gay. We have always loved you. Always. No matter what!" Billie Gay raised her head and looked at her grandmother and something desperate and sorrowful flew across her face like the shadow of a bird. Tears rose in her eyes.

"I'm sorry, Mimma," she whispered in a broken voice. "I'm so sorry." She gripped Gay Nell's hand.

Outside the door, the doberman gave a yelp. "Don't you raise your head to me!" Dwight's voice cut into the room. He flung open the door, dressed in black jeans and a studded black belt and a tee shirt that said "Bad Boy Leather."

"What are you doin' in here—feeding her with a spoon? We're running late." Billie Gay's face closed like a folding door as she dropped Gay Nell's hand and allowed herself to be hustled out of the room by Dwight.

As soon as she heard the car leave, Gay Nell pulled herself up. The time had come. She hauled out the Bible, took the bowl of Beanie-Weenies in her lap and began to stuff the small, blue sleeping pills into the slick hot dog pieces. Two pills could fit in one piece—six pieces, twelve pills. That should be enough. She wiped the gooey brown sauce off of the little pieces of meat with the end of her sheet, took aim, and one by one, slung the pieces under the door. One by one, she heard the doberman gulp them down. She was in good form. None of the pieces stuck to the floor.

She wiped her hands again, and then took out pen and pad and began to write. "Dear Brendan Dunn or Whom It May Concern, All these drugs belong to Dwight Poole. If I survive, I will explain how

Billie Gay and I were held here by him against our will. I am in my right mind. Gay Nell Soames." She folded the note and stuck it in the empty glass pill bottle, then put on the cap and screwed it tight.

She knew she should eat something for strength, but could only choke down half of the soggy bagel and a few gulps of coffee before she struggled up with her walker. She was breathing hard and nervous as a cat.

She put the pill bottle with the note in the walker's white plastic basket, then collapsed the Grab-It down as short as it would go and stuck it in. She rolled into the bathroom where she took the glass chimney off the oil lamp and set it aside. She put the base of the lamp carefully down in the basket and placed the matches beside it.

As she turned back to the bedroom, she heard the sound that she had been waiting for—a low groaning noise from the other side of the door. The pills are beginning to take effect. She heard the doberman get to his feet, take a few steps, and then collapse with a snort. She made her way to the door and slowly cracked it open. The doberman was lying about four feet away at the head of the stairs on his side. His eyes were closed and a thread of saliva dripped onto the floor from his open mouth.

Pushing the walker as fast as she dared, she went on out the door and turned into the second bedroom. It was a mess, clothes strewn around, the bed unmade and the beautiful rose carpet stained. But thank goodness, the phone was still there, sitting on the nightstand. She closed the door behind her, took out the Grab-It and painstakingly lifted the clothes out of her path as she inched toward the closet.

In the closet, Dwight's few, long-sleeved shirts were hanging neatly up on hangers, while Billie Gay's clothes lay in a jumble on the floor. She pushed his clothes aside and bent forward to open the secret compartment on the back wall. The door squeaked open. Jackpot! The area was piled with plastic bags full of white powder. A glass pipe, tubes and syringes sat in an open box with a thin piece of rubber hose coiled around them like a snake. A pain shot into Gay Nell's temples as she looked at this evidence of Billie Gay's downfall. She wanted to take the Grab-It and smash it into the pile of bags, fling them to the floor, rip them open. She saw herself beating the pipe and tubes into tiny shards.

Instead she took a series of long, deep breaths. In a sing-song voice, she intoned, "I-don't-give-a-shit." Then, with the Grab-It, she lifted five of the bags, the pipe and one syringe into her basket. She rolled her way to the window and slid up the screen. The air felt like a piece of heaven on her skin. She leaned out and sighted the goldfish pond. Yep, just about underneath me, easy shot. One by one, she dropped down the bags, the pipe, the syringe, then the glass pill bottle with the note. They all hit the target except the syringe. It glanced off of a rock and lay on the patio. The rest disappeared into the dark water with a froth of bubbles. "Oh, yes!" Gay Nell said under her breath.

The phone call was next. She dialed the memorized number.

"Sheriff's office."

She took a breath. "May I speak to Mr. Brendan Dunn?"

"Speaking." He sounded the same: steady, dependable.

"Hello, Brendan. This is Mrs. Gay Nell Soames. I need to talk to you."

There was a long pause. "Mrs. Soames, Billie Gay's grandma? I thought you were...well... I'm glad to hear from you. Can I help you with something?"

"You most certainly can. Listen carefully. My house is on fire and you've got to get out here right away. "

"What?"

"Listen to me! Billie Gay and I have been held hostage by a drug dealer. Look in the goldfish pond for all the evidence you need! You do remember where the goldfish pond is?"

"Well, yes mam'... but..."

"Nothing is her fault! Look in the fishpond. That's all you have to remember. Now get out here. I hope I'll meet you in the front yard."

"But..."

"GET OUT HERE!"

Gay Nell slammed down the phone. She was shaking. Time was running out. She wanted to be sure the house was ruined before Billie Gay and Dwight got back, so even if the law didn't catch him, he would leave Billie Gay alone.

Gay Nell turned toward the door. She thought she heard a noise outside in the hall. She waited. Nothing. It must be her nerves.

"I don't give a shit," she whispered. She pulled the oil lamp base out of the basket and unscrewed the top where the white wick stuck through. She threw the top and the dripping wick onto the bed and dribbled some more of the reddish oil onto the bedspread which trailed on the floor. To push back feelings of grief and panic she repeated, "I don't give a shit," over and over like a mantra as she slowly circled the room with her walker, splashing oil onto the curtains, the rug, the clothes that still lay on the floor. The smell of the oil made her nauseated but soon the lamp was empty. She stood next to the door and looked back at the room. Billie Gay was a little girl in this room. Her eyes teared up as she reached behind her, opened the door and backed out of it. Holding it open with her walker, she struck a match, lit the entire matchbook and flung it onto the bed. Immediately flames leaped up. She backed into the hall and slammed the door with a bang.

As Gay Nell swung her walker around to launch herself toward the elevator chair, she heard a low growl. The doberman was crouched at the top of the stairs, his long teeth bared, his black hair standing up along his spine. Around his front feet pooled a circle of yellow vomit speckled with bits of Beanie-Weenie. He staggered a bit to one side, but his eyes drilled into Gay Nell like spikes.

Before Gay Nell could move, he sprang. She jerked the walker up towards him, then stumbled and fell heavily on her side. The aluminum legs knocked the dog off his course, but he gathered himself up and leaped at her again. Things seemed to move in slow motion as Gay Nell watched his open jaws come toward her through the air. As though by instinct, she grabbed her left leg and hefted it up. Her blackened foot rose up to catch squarely inside the doberman's mouth with a squishing sound. The dog's eyes bulged in surprise. Then he landed, bit down on her foot and jerked backwards. Gay Nell watched her rotten flesh slide off the bones like a glove. The force of the pull tumbled the doberman backward down the stairs. There was a muffled cracking sound and then nothing.

For a long moment Gay Nell held her breath, staring at her mutilated foot. She could see the white of her toe bones shining in the darkened flesh. There was little pain and only a slow ooze of blood. Then the smell of smoke jarred her into action. Panting, she gathered herself up on hands and knees and half-crawled, half-dragged herself to the top of the stairs. Looking down, she saw the inert body of the doberman lying part way down the steps, his head cocked up at an impossible angle against the wooden banister rails. She heard herself whimper as she slowly drew herself up into the elevator chair.

Smoke was puffing out from under the second bedroom door, unfurling its haze into the hallway. She clicked the switch and the chair began its measured, whirring descent. She held on to the chair with one hand and put the other in front of her nose to filter the smoke. "Hurry, hurry, faster, faster!" She hoped Billie Gay had left the walker in its usual place tucked beside the stairway. If not, she would crawl to the front door. She had already proven today how strong she was.

Abruptly, halfway down, the elevator chair stopped. The whirring sound continued but the chair ceased to move. Gay Nell peered down through the skim of smoke and saw the doberman's head, her own flesh protruding from his mouth, wedged between the bottom of the chair and the stairs. The chair was stuck on the doberman. He had won.

Not now. Not now! Not when I'm almost... With a great cracking sound, flames blew out the second bedroom door. As a wall of heat came toward her, Gay Nell threw up her arms and toppled sideways off the chair. Her face grazed the coarse fur of the dog as she flopped and tumbled down the staircase, bounced off the bottom step and landed on her stomach in front of the French doors, her head facing the glass. After a long moment Gay Nell tried to rise and then realized that her eyes were the only body parts that she could move. The fire snapped and spit in the upstairs hall, and smoke was seeping, in delicate curls, past her head. She looked beyond the French doors and scanned the driveway, her eyes rolling rapidly back and forth. No movement, no one, nothing. She willed herself to move anything, a finger, a toe. Nothing. She slowly allowed her eyes to close. Tears seeped from behind the closed lids and, strangely enough, she thought of the doberman, how in the end they were companions, after all.

Her eyes sprang open again at the sound of a siren. She had the perfect view to see the fire truck wail up the long driveway, the Sheriff's car close behind with flashing dome lights. The vehicles spun to a halt and men swarmed from the fire truck. Brendan Dunn and the Sheriff jumped from his car and the Sheriff straightaway went around back of the house to the fishpond.

Here! I'm here! Surely someone will find me. Yes! Brendon is coming up the porch steps. But no, the firemen stopped him and pushed him back into the yard. The fire hoses sprang to life and the men began to soak the house. Sheets of water streamed over the French doors, so that Gay Nell seemed to be watching the scene outside from behind a waterfall. Never! They'll never find me now. But it wasn't too blurry to see Dwight's car come roaring up the drive, or Billie Gay tearing out of the door before the car stopped.

"Mimma! Mimma!" Billie Gay cried as she ran toward the house. But she was stopped and held by Brendan Dunn's arms. She struggled, and then collapsed onto his chest. The firemen moved around to the back of the house and Gay Nell could see clearly as the Sheriff returned with all the goodies from the goldfish pond. At a nod from Brendan, he approached Dwight, who was standing there cursing under his breath. When Dwight saw what the Sheriff was holding, he tried to run back to his car, but the Sheriff caught him and pushed him up against the hood. Brendan was still cradling Billie Gay's head against his chest and she had both arms around his back.

As Gay Nell watched the drama outside unfold, a new feeling began to come over her, a feeling so powerful, so sweet, touching her as gently as the tip of the curl of smoke she was beginning to take in through her nostrils. Everything is working out. I did it! I saved Billie Gay from the thrall of Dwight and the drugs!

By the time the Sheriff pulled out his cuffs and slipped them on Dwight's wrists, Gay Nell was feeling so good she didn't even care that the thickening smoke was singeing the inside of her nose. I did it! I rode the train all the way to the caboose!

The funny thing was, as soon as she realized that, she began to lose interest in the scene outside. It seemed like a movie she was watching, but was no longer a part of. Even the colors started to grow pale, or maybe that was just the pall of smoke. Whatever it was, she didn't care as much anymore, and that surprised her.

She shut her eyes and drew in more smoke, but it didn't bother her nose now. In fact, it felt smooth and good. It seemed to flow right up through her nostrils into her brain and form a swirl there, a shimmering spiral. Deep inside that spiral, another scene was slowly forming. It was a picture of the curve of Shamrock creek as it lay against the bank. The light under the trees glowed as brightly as if a million stars had gathered there. It pulled her like a beacon, like nothing had ever done before. "Come," it whispered, "Come." But she had already turned toward the creek, where the fresh smell of water rose off the warm rocks, where the rustle of azalea mingled with the sough of pine, where Pig was waiting.

Trip to Seychelles

The harsh antiseptic stung my nose as the doctor stitched up the slash in my lower arm. The bite was long and sinuous, like a stretched out "S."

"It must have been a snake eel since you say you were swimming near the river mouth. They're found in brackish water. Two inches closer, it would have hit your inner wrist, been a bloody mess," the doctor surmised.

He clipped the last stitch. "Kerubo will give you an antibiotic injection and you're good to go. It will heal faster without a bandage, but no more swimming. Come back if it gets inflamed; sometimes in the tropics things are slow to heal." He nodded on his way out.

Kerubo's gaze lingered on my wound. Her long brown face and round black eyes seemed familiar. But that was impossible. I had never been to the Seychelles islands before. Although I knew, because of my job, that the US had installed an Air Force satellite tracking station here in 1963. My work for the last sixteen years had been repairing the large, concave satellite tracking dishes in many countries. I was one of two women who held the job and people were always surprised when I showed up.

I was excited to visit these islands off the coast of Africa. I loved my work, but often felt like a wanderer with no deeper purpose. Having grown up in Florida, I was at home in tropical settings. My grandmother, Oma, had been a Seminole Indian, and we had swum the sea and edges of the mangrove swamps while she taught me about the fish and sea creatures. Whenever I was near the ocean, I felt compelled to explore the waters. This morning, the eel had come from nowhere, darted at me, slashed and wriggled away.

Kerubo continued to stare at me while she gave my shot. Then she fumbled a phone out of her pocket and said, "I can take picture of your mark?"

"Mark? Well sure, if that's what you want."

She took several photos. As she raised her arms, I noticed a tattoo near her inner wrist, smaller but almost the exact shape as my eel bite. When I left she was pounding out a number on her phone.

I ate a tepid lunch at my hotel before driving up through dense jungle to the satellite tracking station. Surprisingly, only one person was there. I was doubly surprised when the small, dark woman who introduced herself as Nuru looked similar to Kerubo. I noticed her focus on my wound before she led me to the computer that controlled the satellite dish.

The only glitch I found was that whenever the satellite swept a certain area of the sky it went blank, then started up again. Very Strange. I never had a problem like this before. Checking my charts, I realized it always went blank over the Lagrange 5 point. Lagrange 5 was a stable point in space in its own orbit between the earth and moon, not influenced by the gravitational pull of any other planet. I knew scientists had long considered it to be a viable point to place a space station.

When I mentioned this to Nuru, she said we would confer with the other members of her crew the next day. She seemed more interested in talking to me about local customs, and asked if I would like to see some native dances that were not open to the public. I agreed and she told me she would pick me up later that evening.

"Tonight is full moon. We will show you how to jump into the moon!" she said, laughing.

"Jump into the moon." Why did that phrase sound so familiar?

I suddenly remembered as I drove away. It was part of a song I had heard Oma sing. I realized that's why these women looked so familiar, they reminded me of her, dark and quick and sensual. My mother and I, with our red hair and freckles, had taken after the Irish side of the family. Though I hadn't had a lot of time with her, Oma and I had shared a deep affection and affinity. When she died suddenly several years ago, there had not been a wake or a funeral. My mother said it was a custom of her tribe, but it left me with a strange feeling of being incomplete.

Nuru arrived at eight-thirty with three other women who had her dark skin and eyes. I was not surprised one of them was Kerubo. As we drove, they explained they had all come to the Islands from Kenya and had brought over their native dances. We parked in a remote part of the island and took a path through dark jungle striped with moonlight. They began to chant in their African language. The sound of insects and night birds wove through their plaintive song. The phrase "jump into the moon" was repeated in English over and over like a refrain. I began to feel entranced by their chanting. It curled around me and drew me through the jungle like a needle drawing thread.

At last we came out into an open space. The full moon glinted off the smooth rocks under our feet. They led me to a large opening in the rocks, and looking down, I saw a natural grotto, full of dark water. My breath caught as I saw, floating in the center of the water, the round, yellow disk of the moon. Other small, dark women were waiting for us. They began to circle the rim of the grotto, chanting and I began to move with them. At the refrain, "jump into the moon," one by one the women jumped into the grotto, shattering the moon's reflection into sharp shards of light. Finally it was only Nuru and myself. I hesitated. Nuru gave me a gentle pat and I jumped – into the moon.

The water was cool and the brackish taste of salt was somehow comforting. After Nuru jumped, I noticed the women were silently swimming through a crack in the rock and following a watery channel. We swam after them and entered into a second large, round chamber where light glowed from the pods of plants that draped against the walls. The chamber was full of women, some stayed in the water and others curled onto rock shelves that lay alongside. One woman swam forward and grasped my hands, pulling me up onto a rock ledge. I looked at her and was stunned.

"Oma?" I whispered.

She caressed my face. "We can take many forms, but yes, I am your Oma. As your grandmother I planted the seeds in you that I hoped would lead you to us someday."

I felt as though I were caught in a dream. "Here? I don't understand. What is this place? Is it really you? I...I thought you were dead."

She drew me close. "Your mother and I thought it best that way. We, all of us here, are of the eel tribe, one of the many tribes of the sea people. We have lived in these oceans since they were first formed. We have been coming from the sea to help you humans since your kind

came to this planet. Do you recall a book I gave you on the Minoan civilization, where the artifacts are mostly of women and dolphins?"
My heart pounding in my ears, I barely managed to whisper, "Yes."

She chuckled. "That was a time when we were most intertwined, when we all worked together for the good of the planet. Many native cultures were aware of our teachings. We are even able to exchange forms if necessary. Did you ever wonder where the idea of mermaids came from? Why dolphins and gigantic whales seem to be eager to connect with humankind?"

I didn't know how to respond.

"But all that is changing now, little one. The worst of mankind has come into power and has poisoned the sea. Our teachings of harmony with nature are lost. Our home as we know it is fast disappearing." She pressed her palm to my heart. "As yours is..."
I knew she spoke truth.

She looked deep into my eyes. "That's where you come in. You were made for this job, and the eel's mark has verified your mission." All around me there was an excited murmuring. As I glanced around, the women's faces and bodies seemed to morph and shift. Was that an eel's pointed snout, the curl of a muscular body, the shimmer of dark, slick skin? Was I going mad? I blinked, and the faces of the women settled in again.

Oma continued, "We have chosen a nearby point in space to create a new world..."

I suddenly understood. "Lagrange 5!" I shouted.

"My, you are a fast learner." She took my hands. "Your mission at this time is to travel to all the satellite scanners and fix the computers so that they seamlessly go past the Lagrange 5 points without detecting anything. By the time it is noticed, our new world will be complete and we will be dwelling there."

"But how will I get access to...?"

"The way is already paved for you. As I said, we take many forms when necessary. Many are waiting to work with you."

"But will I...?

She read my thoughts. "Yes, you will be able to come live with us if you choose. We will create a new world similar to this one and will be teaching the ways of living in harmony with nature. You and I will once again swim together in another sea. If other women wish to learn our ways, they can study with us, and also return to try and heal this planet. If it is not too late."

"But..."

Oma pressed her fingers to my lips, then lifted my arm and placed a kiss on my wound. "Sleep now, little one. My love always surrounds you."

I felt myself falling backwards into darkness. Many soft bodies seemed to bear me up.

I awoke in my hotel bed, morning sun slanting across the spread. My body was sore but a new sense of purpose glowed inside my chest. My mind grappled with remembering the strange dream I had. I stretched out my arms and, glancing upward, saw that my wound was no longer there. In its place, dark and sinuous, was the perfectly shaped tattoo of an eel.

༩∞ལ

Blue

When I was six we lived in Forge Gap, Virginia, a railroad town set in the crack where two mountains came together. Forge Mountain was on one side and Sweet Mountain on the other, and the railroad ran between them. We lived outside of town in a big yellow farmhouse. We had an oak grove and a chicken house and a crazy uncle that lived across the "circle." The "circle" was a smooth, round stretch of clay where we built castles and learned to ride our bikes. Uncle Miller lived on the other side. He was fifty-two years old and he went crazy when his wife died and he had a stroke and started drinking too much Bromo Seltzer. In his back yard was a pile of old blue Bromo Seltzer bottles that was taller than I was. My sister and I would go over and collect any blue bits of glass that had broken and put them in jars with other colored pieces we'd found. Then Miller would fill the jars with water and put tops on them. We'd hold them up to the light and turn them round and round. "Kaleidoscope," my sister would say, matter-of-factly, and Miller and I would nod our heads. My sister was sick a lot and read piles of books about things I had never even heard of. Besides, she was eight.

One afternoon she was showing me how to build a moat around my castle, when we heard Miller call, "Hey-ooo!"

"Hey-ooo!" we called back. That was a signal. It meant Miller was hiding and we had to find him. It had come from the grove, so we ran in that direction. Bea found him. He had lain in the green and white striped hammock and pulled both sides up over himself. Miller was a tall man with a lot of black hair that hung in his eyes. Sometimes his bones seemed too big, like they were about to poke out through his skin and he walked kind of funny, with one leg slower than the other. The sides of the hammock didn't quite cover him.

"Miller, you're just like an Egyptian Mummy!" Bea exclaimed. Before I could ask her to explain, Miller sat up and said, "Go ask your mama if y'all can come to the cemetery with me. I got somethin' to show you!"

The town cemetery was just back of the grove and through a small patch of woods. We often went there with Miller and collected bits of ribbon and withered flowers off the graves, but we always had to ask. I ran into the kitchen where Mama was bending over the dishpan.

"Can we, Mama?"

She smiled and wiped the brown hair off her forehead with the back of her hand. "All right, if Miller's goin'." I started off.

"Dora."

"Yes, Mama?"

"You tell Miller to carry Bea if she gets tired."

Miller had already swung Bea up to his shoulders. He liked to carry her around and do things to protect her. He said she was like a little snowflake and if we didn't protect her, she might melt clean away. He grabbed my hand and we set off through the grove.

"What is it, Miller. Is it a new grave?" Bea kicked her feet against Miller's chest.

"Y'all jus' wait now. We'll be there soon enough."

I swung hard on his hand. "Will we like it, Miller? Do you like it?"

"Oh I like it and you're gonna like it, and that's for sure." Miller's eyes were bright.

"Is it another statue? Is it another lamb statue, Miller?" I asked.

Miller laughed. "Okay, I'll tell you one thing. It is a statue, but it ain't no statue of a lamb!"

The lamb statue was one of our favorite things. It was gray concrete with a curly green fungus growing down its sides that looked just like wool. Sometimes we'd tie ribbons on its neck while Miller told us the story of the lost lamb from the Bible

Just before we reached the cemetery, Miller stopped. "Now both of you close your eyes. Close them tight now and don't look till I tell you. Promise you won't!"

"We won't. We promise!"

Miller dragged me forward. His hand got tighter and tighter on mine. Finally he stopped.

"Okay!" he almost shouted, "Okay, here she is!"

I opened my eyes and looked up. She was so big. Taller than me, taller than Miller, taller than Bea on Miller's shoulders. The sunlight sparkled and bounced off the bosom of the biggest, whitest, most beautiful angel I had ever seen.

"Oh, Miller!" Bea whispered.

I didn't say anything. I just stared at her and forgot to breathe. Miller lifted Bea down and stepped over to the statue. He reached up and put his hand over one of her white ones. "This here," he announced grandly, "this here is Janet Kalvey, and she is a friend of mine!" That broke the spell.

"How do you know her, Miller?"

"Can we touch her?"

"Look at her wings!"

"She's so beautiful!"

Miller was pacing around her, touching the folds in her skirt and the tips of her wings. He had begun to sweat.

"You see those wings?" he said. "Every night when the sun goes down, those wings begin to move and when it's dark she puts up her arms..." Miller put his arms up... "and her wings begin to move..." he flapped his arms, "...and she flies right up to heaven, to God hisself!" Miller gave a crooked leap and threw back his head. Then he whispered, "But she has to be back, back before the sun comes up again, just like this." He stroked her skirt. "Cold and still, so no one will know."

Bea was staring at Miller with a funny look on her face. Then she turned to me. "Let's decorate her!" she cried.

We scampered from grave to grave collecting faded ribbon and flowers that "showed brown," as Mama said. Miller lifted me up to drape pink ribbons over the crests of her wings while Bea made a flower necklace for her head. For a special touch, Miller took an empty blue Bromo Seltzer bottle out of his pocket and laid it in the crook of her arm. The sun came through the bottle and made a patch of blue on her white marble bosom.

Then Miller crouched on the ground in front of us. "You know the best thing about Janet Kalvey?" We shook our heads. "I'll tell you what the best thing is. If you have any kind of problem, or if you're jus' lonesome, you can come down here and tell Janet Kalvey, and that night she'll take your problem right up to heaven. Right up to God hisself. And if He can't fix things, then nobody can! That's the very best thing," he said.

"How do you know that, Miller?" Bea said.

"How do I know?" He looked up at the statue. "I know because she told me so. That's how I know."

Bea stood still. "I want to go home now," she said. "It's time to get Queenie."

Miller stood up and passed his hand over his face. "Let me carry you."

"No, I'll walk," said Bea. She darted toward the path and we followed.

Queenie was Bea's pet hen. She was fat and golden and wouldn't lay with the other hens in the chicken house. Every day about three o'clock she'd run up and down inside the fence until Bea came and opened the gate. Then she'd fly into Bea's arms and Bea would take her to the tool shed where she had her own private nest in an old Coca-Cola crate. She sometimes laid eggs with double yolks. Mama said she was the best layer we had.

At supper, we told Mama and Papa about Miller and Janet Kalvey. Mama laughed. "Crazy Miller, I believe he did know Janet Kalvey. Didn't he do some kind of work for her, hauling wood or something? Imagine her family being able to afford such a headstone."

Papa banged down his butter knife. "Hauling wood and every other thing. And it was my tools and tractor he used to borrow to go work for her. I saw them once riding together in that old rattletrap truck of his. Her car must have broke down. I swear, Evelyn, I wish you wouldn't allow him around the girls so much. He gets more peculiar all the time."

"Now, Charles, you know he'd rather die than hurt the girls. Why, he looks after them and plays with them. Besides, since Aunt Jenny died, they're one of his few joys in this world."

"Sure they are!" Papa scraped back his chair. "Them and his Bromo Seltzer bottles! That's just not natural. Sometimes I think he would be better off if he took to drinking what other men drink..."

"Charles!" Mama glanced as us, then sharply back at him.

That night Bea and I lay listening to the trains rustling and hissing over in the train yard. I raised on one elbow. "What's 'peculiar' mean?"

Bea was staring into the dark. "I don't know. Go to sleep."

"I'm not sleepy. What do 'other men' drink?"

"Whiskey."

"What color bottles does it come in?"

She turned away from me. "I'm going to sleep now."

The next day Miller shot Papa's best bird dog. It was really Queenie's fault. Everyone was gone except me and Miller. He was teaching me to whittle on the back porch. Under the porch was Papa's dog, Sheba, and her new litter of five pups that she hadn't let anyone get near yet.

Miller looked up. "There she goes." Queenie was running up and down the fence. I got up. I didn't like to take Queenie to the shed, but she would only go with Bea or with me. She usually pecked me quite a bit. Bea said it was from disappointment. That day she pecked me so hard I threw her down and she ran under the porch. I ran after her. She ran right into Sheba's puppies and they cried and Sheba jumped up and bit the nearest thing, which was me, and I cried, and Miller got Papa's gun and shot Sheba and all of her puppies. He made me go to my room, but I knew that's what he was doing. I counted the shots. Then Papa came driving up and that's when all the shouting started.

That night Bea and I got out of bed and went into Mama and Papa's room to open the heat grate so we could hear them taking downstairs. Papa was pacing in and out of our view. "I will not have him over here destroying my property. I will not! He shoots the best dog I ever owned, he fills my children's heads with nonsense, he..."

"Charles," we could see Mama's hands lying flat on the table. "He didn't mean to destroy anything. He was just trying to protect Dora. He told you that."

"Protect! If he knows so much about protect, why didn't he know Sheba was just protecting her pups? But no, all he could think of with that fogged brain of his was rabies. Rabies! I can't believe it! Surely he knew she'd had her shots! And the bite hardly broke the skin!"

"Well, Charles, there are a lot of rabies cases in the county."

"But why didn't he wait? Why did he kill them all? I had promised every one of those pups to friends of mine."

"Well, he didn't wait, and you're just wearing yourself out with it, and me too." Mama sounded mad.

"Okay, okay, I'll stop. But I don't want him over here anymore. I want it broken off! And that's that. Do you hear?"

"But Charles..."

"No 'buts' Evelyn. No 'buts' this time!"

Bea pulled my nightgown and led me back to bed. Her hands were so small, smaller than mine even, and very hot. The windows were open and the peepers down by the creek were singing. They were so loud that their noise felt like it came from inside me.

"Bea, are you asleep?"

"No."

"Does that mean we can't play with Miller anymore?"

Her thin fingers gripped mine under the sheet. "I don't know," she said.

"But you've got to know." I said. "You always know."

"I don't know," she said. She began to cry.

We didn't see Miller for a week. Mama said he was visiting relatives in Parksburg. Then one morning I woke up and knew he was back. I don't know how I knew it. I just did. Bea was already up, crouching by the window. The sun came right through her blonde hair like it wasn't even there. I kneeled beside her and we watched Miller carry a box of trash into his backyard.

"Why is he walking like that, so slow?" I whispered.

"I think...maybe he's tired from his trip."

"Let's go ask him. Come on."

Mama was in the doorway. She drew us close and smoothed our hair. "You can't see Miller today. He's not...feeling well. If he wants to see you, he'll come here. Do you understand?" Mama looked funny. "Now, I've got a new game for you, downstairs."

Days passed and Miller didn't come for us. But he did other things. Things we learned of by way of the heat grate at night. He stole Papa's sweet corn and sold it to some people 'over town.' He carried Mama's big black soup pot out of the grove and put it up in a tree down in the woods. He took to putting his coat over his head and jumping out at people in the cemetery. But it was the night after he had torn the wires loose in Papa's tractor that my Papa's voice sounded so strangely quiet.

"That's it, Evelyn. He's going. I'll take him or I'll call them to come for him, but he's going."

"Yes, Charles. You're right."

"And you keep the children away from him until he's gone. You don't know what he'll do next. You understand?"

"Yes. I just wish..." She sighed.

"You wish what?"

"Nothing. You're right. It's time."

Back in our rooms we knelt by the window and stared across at Miller's lights. Our room was very hot and the peepers were too loud again. Suddenly, Bea stood up. "We've got to," she said. Her eyes glistened in the dark.

"What? Got to what?"

"Janet Kalvey." she whispered. She seemed to be thinking to herself.

"The marble angel?" I grew excited. "We'll ask her to go up to God and ask help for Miller?"

"We've got to. It's all I can think of."

"Now?"

"No, tomorrow."

"But Mama won't let us go by ourselves..." I began.

"We'll tell her something else. We'll tell her we're going in the grove to play hide and seek."

"Bea, will it work?"

She turned away from me. "Of course it will. Didn't Miller say so?"

The next day we were so quiet, Mama asked if we were sick. We told her we weren't. We planned to go right after Bea took Queenie to the tool shed. I waited at the edge of the grove. Bea left Queenie in the Coca-Cola crate and crossed the yard to Mama at the clothesline. I could almost see her speak the words.

Mama nodded and Bea started toward me.

And then it happened. There was huge explosion from the shed. Glass and pieces of board flew into the air and great orange flames started leaping from the windows and roof.

"Queenie!" Bea's high voice cried, "Queenie!" over and over as she ran toward the flames.

Mama threw down the wash and ran. "No, Bea, Bea, Bea, no!" Mama screamed.

I was running too, but my legs were so slow and then another explosion shook the shed and flames boiled out onto Bea's clothes and hair and she was screaming. Mama threw herself on Bea and they rolled over and over. Then something seemed to tear apart inside me and I fell down into darkness.

————————

When I woke up, I was in our bed and Aunt Anna, from "over town" was sitting beside me. She said I shouldn't worry, that Bea had something called "skin grafts" and Mama had "third degree burns" but the doctors were taking care of everything. She said of course Miller had done it and that everyone was looking for him, even the police, and I should drink this medicine and go back to sleep. I drank something bitter and brown and as soon as she went downstairs, I got up and sneaked out the back way.

It was almost sunset. I had to hurry. The peepers were starting up as I ran through the grove. My head was dizzy, but my body felt so light I didn't even seem to touch the ground. By the time I reached the cemetery, the sun was coming off the top of Sweet Mountain so red I could hardly see.

Janet Kalvey's wings were tipped with red as they rose high above the other tombstones, an orangey-red, and it seemed to me they moved. As I got close, I saw a dark shape climbing right up on her. It was Miller. He had hold of one of her arms and he was scrambling with one leg while his slow leg hung loose. His face was on her bosom and he was crying and making funny sounds like I'd never heard before. He turned and saw me and dropped to the ground. He came and knelt down in front of me and took my shoulders and put his face close to mine. "I didn't do it," he said. "I didn't, I didn't do it."

Suddenly I was hitting him, over and over, as hard as I could. I felt his soft wet face under my fists and I could hear a whimpering animal sound, but I didn't know if it was Miller or me. And all the while he seemed to get smaller and smaller at the end of a black tunnel that kept closing in, blacker and blacker, with Miller at the end. Then I put my head back and saw her, and she smiled down at me and her wings WERE moving, slow and sweet in the evening light. She bent over me and I felt her lift me in her arms. "Up to heaven, right up to God hisself." I turned in towards her and slept.

———————

I could tell by the way the sun lay on our bed it was afternoon. Something was throbbing behind my eyes and I heard Papa's voice downstairs. I went to the heat grate. He was talking on the phone.

"...was just standing there with her in his arms. No, no nothing like that...we checked. She's still asleep... No, he didn't even resist. He was like a dead person, wouldn't even speak. They just led him off. Thing was, he didn't set the fire. ...no, it was a frayed wire and those cans of solvent I'd been using. But it had been going on too long. And now all of this..." Papa's voice choked and he stopped talking for a moment. "He should have been taken away long ago."

I walked slowly back to our room. My feet felt funny against the floor, like they were too big, and yet everything in the room looked small, smaller than it ever had before. On the top of the dresser was our kaleidoscope jar. I took it to the window and shook it in the sunlight. The pieces on the top swirled up for a minute and then settled back down. Most of them were blue.

*[Published in **Southern Distinctions**, Oct. 2004]*

ڪيو

Meeting Kan

There were about fifteen people sitting on the floor in a circle when I slipped through the door of the hotel conference room to join the group. We had gathered for the first workshop in a series given by the Foundation for Shamanic Studies. If we completed the eight workshops, we would possess some of the tools used by shamanic people all over the planet to enter other realities and bring back information and healing.

It seemed like we should be sitting out under the sky near some giant trees or rocks instead of this drab maroon and green room that smelled of cleaning products, but I knew from experience that deep learning often happens in strange places.

As I settled on the floor with my pillows and blankets, I scanned the other members of the group. There was a mix of men and women, and most seemed middle aged, as I was. Directly across from me sat a heavyset man in a leather vest. Silver and turquoise rings bunched up on his thick fingers and a necklace of large teeth, (bear, wolf?) hung from his neck. He had bloodshot eyes and an arrogant cock to his head. Beside him hovered a thin blonde dressed in fringes, with her gray hair in braids. I mentally rolled my eyes, hoping he wasn't the shaman. Being a massage therapist, I had pretty good radar for people's energy signatures and he had "pretender" written all over him.

My inner critic piped up. *At a spiritual workshop and already with the judgments, eh?*

I sighed. I was trying to learn how to walk the thin line between judgment and discernment. It was easy to confuse the two.

Another person in the group who caught my attention was a young black woman who had the poise and elegance of royalty while sitting serenely in her multicolored frock. I could easily see her as the shaman. I think we were all surprised when a slim, blonde, bespectacled man in jeans and a plain denim shirt stood up and introduced himself.

Mr. Peepers, the shaman! I breathed a sigh of relief. He spoke in a quiet, confident voice describing the morning's activities, where we would learn to journey to the Lower World and, later, journey again to meet a power animal to be our ally.

We then went around the room, introducing ourselves and speaking about our reasons for coming to the workshop. I was not quite sure what I would say when my turn came. Two years before, when a friend gave me a copy of *The Way Of The Shaman* by Michael Harner, the book seemed somehow familiar. After finishing it, I found everything I could get my hands on, to read about shamanism.

The facts were fascinating. Experts date shamanism as being 30,000 to 45,000 years old, with ancient cave and rock drawings providing clues. The practice started in Siberia and is still in practice there today. The word "shaman" comes from the language of the Evenk, a small Tungus-speaking tribe of hunters and reindeer herding people who live in central Siberia. The word refers to a person who has the ability to "know in an ecstatic manner." The plural form is "shamans." The core tenant of shamanism is the ability of shamans to travel to other levels of reality to bring back knowledge, healing and inspiration for their tribe.

Shamans do not think of these worlds as a part of their own mind, such as the unconscious or the super conscious. To a shaman, these worlds exist independently of the mind. They use their mind as a doorway to reach the other worlds. Primarily, these other worlds are thought to represent the true nature of things, as opposed to this physical world where humans are often in the dark about their own problems, their causes and cures. The other worlds provide explanations and healing, and the shaman's actions in these domains can exert direct influence on this world. These other realms may be filled with guides, spirit animals, sacred places, ancestors, and magical objects.

Some historians propose that shamanism is the forerunner of all religious thought and the shamanic belief in souls traveling to other worlds set the stage for the Christian belief in heaven and hell. Although the Russian Orthodox Church, Buddhists and Communists have attacked shamanism at different periods in history, it retains its original concepts.

One of the things that spoke to me was the fact that shamanism imbues the natural world with spirit or energy. Each rock, stone and animal is said to have its own essence or "medicine" that can interact with humans in powerful ways. The natural world was one of the true loves of my life, instilled in me first by my father and then through my own experiences. I often thought of Frank Lloyd Wright's quote, "I believe in God. Only I call it Nature".

I introduced myself simply as someone who loved nature and wanted to find out more about shamanism. This would be the first experiential part of my study.

Harner was an anthropologist who traveled the world studying shamanic practitioners and wrote about his travels among native peoples. He found such value in shamanic techniques that he formed the Foundation for Shamanic Studies to assure that these teachings do not die out. The Foundation also teaches "core shamanism" which Harner had assimilated from different tribes. As part of our self-help culture, he believed people could be taught shamanic tools to use in helping themselves and others in this modern century. This part of the trend, called "neo-shamanism" has filtered down into our present day world—into psychology, the arts, self-help programs, spiritual systems, and even medicine, for now scientists are studying many of the plants long known to shamans for their healing potential.

After a short break, we lay on our blankets and pillows to prepare for the first shamanic journey as the shaman had instructed us. With our eyes closed, we would journey in our imaginations to the Lower World, one of four destinations for the shaman; the others being the Middle, Upper and Upper Upper Worlds. To do this, we would find a place in nature where we felt comfortable and look for an opening: a hole in the ground, a knot on a tree, the bottom of a spring. In our mind's eye, we would enter the opening, making ourselves very small if necessary, and travel downward through the earth. At the end of our journey we would come out into the Lower World, which might look different for each individual. We'd look around and get comfortable with the place, before coming back through our tunnel to this level of reality.

From my reading, I knew these worlds were thought to be not imaginary, but imaginal, existing in a realm of experience where they inhabit a reality of their own. After returning to this earthly world we could write about the experience in our notebooks to share later if we wished. To travel, we would "ride" the sound of the shaman's drum into the Lower World. The shaman beats the drum in a cadence of three to four drumbeats per second for the journey. Four sets of faster drumbeats call you back from the imaginal land to this earthly place.

Someone asked, "How do we know it won't just be our imaginations and not a real journey?"

The shaman replied with a kind smile, "How do you know your imagination isn't a journey?"

Before he began drumming, the shaman laid out his power bundle: a beautiful pouch decorated with feathers and beads, a spiral of seashells and some spotted stones. He taught us some simple chants to call the spirits and proceeded to call the energies of the four directions, East, South, West, North and some of his own personal guides. I made myself comfortable with pillows at my head and beneath my knees and a dark cloth over my eyes to block out all the light.

The drumming began and I knew where I was going. In my mind's eye I began my route to a cave that was in a neighboring county in the Virginia Mountains where I lived. A friend had introduced me to the cave the year before, and I often took people there to explore and feel the thrill of being deep underground.

The religions of many cultures have ways of accessing spiritual energy, becoming entranced, altered and high without drugs. Many of the methods of eliciting these feelings start with ritual repetitive sound and movement: Jewish davening, percussive singing, chanting of the Gyuoto Monks, the dancing and spinning of the whirling dervishes, the fasting or drumming of many native cultures. The physical traditions of ritual and ceremony can also elicit these states, as in traditional Catholic ceremonies.

Christianity in America has little of this opportunity to trance, unless you go to a Pentecostal church where people may be encouraged to feel the spirit in their bodies and speak in tongues. Raised in the rather dry Presbyterian Church, I was longing for something more immersive. I relaxed and let the drum rhythm carry me toward the cave.

It was dark. Sinking Creek murmured low on my right as I walked up the road with a steep mountainside heaving up on my left. I put on my headlamp as I walked. The gibbous moon illuminated a faint trail snaking upward. I turned and began the climb. The incline was so sharp I had to pull myself up with my hands, using the jagged rocks and some gnarly tree roots. I twisted my body to avoid the drifts of poison ivy that hung onto the path.

The cave's mouth opened as an oblong slit in the rock about three feet high and four feet wide. The cave's breath purled out onto my face, cool and damp. I took the sage I'd gathered in my garden from my pocket and crushed it against the cave's rocky lip. The pungent oils released and mingled with the deep smell of earth as I gave thanks to this place and called protection for myself.

I adjusted my headlamp to "on" and slipped, feet first, through the opening. The damp and dark rushed to hold me. For me, there was always a sense of welcome in this cave. I was comfortable, yet excited. I have always felt at home in the dark. On my left, shallow webs formed from stalagmites and stalactites rose up. When hit by the light, their sides glittered with tiny crystals grown there. A black pit opened in front of me and I followed the trail along the rim, on past the caverns. The trail slanted down toward the pit, and occasionally a bit of scree fell from my boot and reverberated far below. At the one dangerous place, the path became thin and the wall of the cave came out in a point, so I had to hug the wall and swing one leg out and around the point to find a landing, then grip the wall and ease my body around till my other foot found a place. In this journey, I did it easily, almost fluidly. I followed as the trail continued and then meandered down and over some giant boulders. As I reached the bottom, I could hear the murmur of Sinking Creek as it ran through the cave, the water swooping away under low stone overhangs. The trail appeared to end, but at the right place, I stooped down to go under a rock ledge, then stood up into another tall corridor where huge, thick columns of rusty-colored rock lay scattered in the path. I picked my way along, my headlamp making a circle of light just in front of me. I suddenly came out under a domed ceiling into a large, round room we had dubbed the Moon Room. Sinking Creek curved along the edge, flowing so quietly I could hardly hear it. The floor of this room also domed up in a wide hump, and in its center sat a round pool with a rock in the middle. In wet weather, water dripped down from the ceiling into the pool. The taste of wet saturated my mouth.

To find the opening in this journey, I continued to the back wall of the Moon Room. Here the creek flowed out of a fissure in the rock. I stepped one foot into the water, made myself very small, and entered the crack.

I found myself in a narrow tunnel, with reddish earth pressing in on me from all sides. The tunnel was a light reddish-gold color, and there were round, red blobs here and there, looking like giant corpuscles. Hairy, mud-covered roots hung from the sides of the passage. I was not going straight down, but rather at a gentle angle. Feeling like Alice in the rabbit hole, down and down I went. I traveled with ease and there was something comforting about the experience so far. The tunnel lightened and I knew I was approaching the end. The light got brighter and suddenly I burst through a round opening into another world.

I stood in a lush savanna of waving grass and sunshine. Here and there were several squat, umbrella-shaped trees like the ones you see on photos of the plains of Africa. In the distance was the scribble of a copse of some sort of vegetation. The air was light on my skin and a nutty, earthy smell came into my nose. I heard the soft sound of slow water running nearby and, sure enough, a lazy stream snaked its way through the grasses on my left, the sun glinting on the surface. I moved toward the stream, noticing I was back in my full-sized human form. Before I reached the stream, the drumming cadence changed and I was being called back. I returned to the tunnel and traveled up the way I had come down, through the reddish tunnel, the Moon Room, the trail, down the mountainside, and eventually back into the hotel room where I opened my eyes.

It was jarring to be back in the green and maroon hotel room, but a sense of awe for my experience was nestled inside my chest. After a few orienting moments, I rolled over, took up my notebook and began to describe the journey.

We took a short snack and restroom break before we settled back into our places on our blankets to began our second journey. For this journey, the shaman assured us, if the time were right, we would be met in the underworld by an animal that was to be our power animal. A power animal would act as our ally. It would help us navigate the ordinary or the shamanic worlds. Its medicine, or specific energy it carried, might be energy we needed to balance us or just an enhancement of the energy we already had—kind of a cosmic caffeine kick. Since I first heard the words, "power animal," I had wondered what mine would be. The drum began. Down the rabbit hole once again.

I went through the familiar tunnel. The journey was rapid. Mud and red blobs and roots flashed by. When I burst through the opening, there stood a giant polar bear, looking like a cross between a real bear and a soft cartoon bear one might see on a child's greeting card.

As I approached him, the bear faded back and forth, real/cartoon, real/cartoon. When I saw the real bear, his fierceness, his raw strength, I realized he was changing so that I wouldn't be afraid of him—so I would be able to approach. When I drew closer, his smell enveloped me, an aroma by which I have known him ever since—the pristine smell of wind over snow. As I had been instructed, I asked him his name. He lifted his paw to the blue sky and, with one claw, wrote the letters K-A-N. The letters came out fluffy and soft like the contrail of a jet. I whispered his name first, and then addressed him, "Hello. Kan." We stared into each other's eyes for a long moment. The black depths of his eyes were familiar and new at the same time. They pulled me. A dizzy feeling began in the middle of my skull. Kan broke eye contact. He dropped to all fours and motioned with his head for me to climb onto his back. I hesitated, then moved toward him slowly as though in a dream. As I grasped his fur to pull myself up, he turned into full bear—no cartoon here—and the feeling of power under me stirred my senses. His fur was not coarse, but soft and buttery. He was so large and high it was hard to settle into a seat. I leaned forward and grasped his neck as he began to run. His muscles flexed under my legs and I had a moment of panic. What had I gotten myself into this time?

And we were off, traveling faster and faster, the field streaming back on either side. I was barely hanging on, a feeling of exhilaration muffled by one of fear. Then the drum signaled us to return, and suddenly I was back in the tunnel, leaving Kan behind with no transition, scrambling with relief toward the normal world.

After a lunch break, the shaman instructed us how to journey for another person, using our power animal as a guide. We each formed a question for our partner to take to their animal for an answer. I chose the young black woman with the regal bearing, whose name was Luce. Her deep brown eyes were calm as she framed her query, "What should my partner and I do for money?" The question made me nervous. It seemed too reality- based, too materialistic, for questioning a power animal. I was expecting something more along the lines of spiritual seeking or emotional support, something I could fudge an answer to if Kan didn't come through. Then I had to laugh at myself. Here I was, trying to navigate the spirit world with all my human foibles intact. Wanting control, wanting to look good, wanting Kan to look good, willing to fudge to make him look good.

As per the instructions, Luce and I lay beside one another, touching at shoulder and hip, and the drum began. Much to my delight, Kan did not disappoint. He loomed at the end of the tunnel, half real, half cartoon. (Had he known how scared I was on that ride?) I repeated Luce's question. He sat there, looking thoughtful. We had been told to keep the energy of our intention strong, so I spoke it again in a louder voice. The Cartoon Kan turned slowly, lifted his paw and wrote in the sky, again with fluffy, cloud-like script, "Dance to Market."

I waited. "Is that all?" I queried. Kan just sat, looking at me calmly. "That's it? Could you elaborate more? What does it mean?"

Kan morphed into real bear and stared back at me with a ferocious, take-no-prisoners-look. I stepped back, "Okay, okay." I realized that was all I was going to get. I reminded myself to accept and turned back toward the tunnel, then swung around, "Kan, thank you."

The big bear smiled a cartoon smile and closed and opened his eyes slowly the way a cat sometimes does. I've heard this is the way a cat blows you a kiss. Did I just receive a kiss from a power animal?

I was apologetic when I related Kan's message to Luce. Head down, I fiddled with my blanket. "He didn't say much and I know this probably makes no sense, but he said, 'Dance to Market,' with a capital 'M.'"

Luce threw back her head and laughed. "That's awesome! Do you know the two things my partner and I have been talking about? Teaching African dance for kids and selling fruit at the Eastern Market in D.C. Market with a capital 'M'." She leaned toward me. "He was really tapping into us!"

I straightened up and flushed. "Wow. I mean, I thought he was talking nonsense. I didn't really expect.... But which one does it mean?"

"I don't know. Maybe it means do both, or maybe he was just confirming we are on the right track, or... I don't know. Maybe your Animal is just psychic, just picking up my thoughts." She smiled gently and laid a hand on my arm. "Whatever it means, I think the veil was pierced." She rose. "I've got to go find the restroom."

I sat there, the phrase, "the veil was pierced," reverberating in my mind. The veil had been pierced and I had learned an important lesson in receiving help from Kan: trust what he writes in the sky, especially if you don't understand it. Toward the end of the two-day workshop we were all familiar enough with our animals to participate in the finale, which was "dancing our animals." To the beat of the drum we were to call our animals to us, invite them to enter our bodies and allow them to move through us: to spring, or leap or crawl, and to utter their sounds through our throats.

When we adopted the gestures and movements of our animals we hoped to awaken to the essence or energy they carried. It would help shift our perception to understand the consciousness of that particular manifestation of nature. The Eastern practices of Yoga, Taoism, and Kung Fu all contain movements reflecting animals. In the 1984 movie, The Karate Kid, a boy wins the final karate match by using a form called "the crane." He had learned to emulate the energy of a crane waiting to spear a fish. The resulting attributes of balance, patience and attention gave him the winning strike at the end of the match.

For me, the experience became an exercise in elation. It is something I still employ when I need to sip a little power. Besides, I have always loved to dance.

We cleared the room of all workshop debris—pillows and purses and notebooks—and the shaman turned the lights down so low we were hardly visible to one another. He instructed us to find a private space for ourselves in the room. As I found my space, my mind flitted back to my theatre days in college. I remembered how I had enjoyed arching my body as a cat in modern dance and tiptoeing about the stage as a butterfly in acting class. I also recalled my study of guided imagery. My teacher had told us that one way to stay in an altered state was to pay attention to details. "Just like you do in ordinary reality; you look around, touch, taste, smell. You check out how you feel. You notice things." Another key to staying altered is to suspend judgment, to release caring if it's imagination, or longing, or some sort of parallel world, to just stay in the experience.

It took me a while to start to ride the sound of the drum. I felt resistant, as though the pounding noise was beating against a door that didn't want to release. I removed my glasses; glad I was so nearsighted I wouldn't be distracted by the movement of others. Then I closed my eyes and let myself fall. The falling sensation started behind my eyes, then swooped down to my solar plexus and I let go. The sound took me and I was riding it. Kan was there beside me without my calling him. He loomed over me, his cartoon-self gone, the coarse density of his form mitigated only by the kindness in his eyes. Nevertheless, a primal fear crawled up my spine. I had to tell myself, He's me. He's mine. It's safe to be here. Pay attention to the details.

Kan's thick, white fur rippled as though in a breeze. His smell, wind over snow, enveloped me. He waited. Without knowing why, I turned my back to him. My mind spoke, *Come.* With a whispering sound, he entered through the nape of my neck. A tingling sensation ran down my arms. My shoulders rolled back, my chest thrust itself out, my chin up. The feeling swept down my legs and they moved into a wide half-squat. Boom! My hands hit the floor and I was on all fours. Kan snapped into my body like a lid snapping onto Tupperware. I felt as though I was blowing up like a balloon, with muscle and fur rather than air. Physical power churned through me. My neck dropped down and forward. I sensed my shoulders shrug upward and my brow being pushed down to elongate my nose. An unseen hand pulled my jaws out into a bear's muzzle. I fought to stay with the process. I was controlling it, yet not controlling it. I was in collusion with it. If I became conscious of a body part, say my tongue, everything I have ever observed or read about a polar bear's tongue was instantly translated into my tongue and it lolled, wet and long, out of the side of my mouth. I clashed my teeth. Firmly planted on the floor with pillar-like legs, I slowly swung my massive head from side to side. A long, moaning grunt came from my throat. I moved my front feet around to the side and then my back feet. I reared on my back legs and hugged the air with my arms. I bounded across the floor and fell on all fours again. I rolled onto my back and then clambered up. I danced the swaying dance of a large, heavy animal, an animal who seemed to need no one, who ruled in a harsh environment, a beast who could take a person's head off with the casual swat of a paw. I had never experienced these feelings of confidence in my body. I lifted my head and rolled my upper lip back as I unhinged my lower jaw. A roar charged up through the core of my body and shattered into the room. I was sweating. I was bursting with power.

After returning home from the shamanic workshop, I researched the attributes of polar bears in this earthly reality and in the imaginal worlds. Physically, the senses of the polar bear are acute. Having a hundred times more sensors in their noses than humans, they can smell a seal underneath the snow twenty miles away. Their hearing is as sharp as a dog's and some native peoples say that polar bears can see color, unlike most animals. Even though they may weigh more than 1,000 pounds, they can swim 100 miles nonstop in icy waters, run at 40 miles per hour across land and travel ice at half that time. They walk as humans do, heel to toe. Adjusting her metabolism, the female can live off of her fat while her heart slows to eight beats per minute in a winter den with her cubs. They form friendships with other polar bears and exhibit behavior that is characterized as play. Humans are their only enemies.

To the Inuit, the polar bear embodies the spirit of the North and is considered the shamanic keeper of their age-old wisdom. There are myths of humans and bears living together and shape shifting into one another. Some traditions believe the bears are the ghosts of humans who have unfinished business on the earth. One with polar bear energy can walk the paths between worlds with ease and grace. This bear can also teach humans how to be both fierce and playful. When it appears as a power animal, it can signal the beginning of a spiritual journey and the awakening of innate abilities.

Although I never returned to study with The Foundation for Shamanic Studies, as my own life challenges quickened, I continued to journey with Kan to answer questions for myself. With each journey Kan became more real to me and I included him in my morning circle of guides I called upon to see me through my days. If my day was full of challenges, I'd bring him into my body for just a few movements, a few head swings, so I could remember that touch of power later.

For a short time, I practiced journeying to help people with their life choices, but soon found I was often afraid I would misinterpret the words or images Kan presented to me. I did not want to inadvertently misguide or harm someone. Kan had three modes of imparting information: he wrote words in the sky with his claw, his words sounded in my head, (which I called "think/talk,") or he presented an image with a step to the side and a flourish of his paw, like a magician at the zenith of his trick. Sometimes Kan was quite the ham.

But in that brief time when I journeyed for others, I recall two journeys in particular that helped me realize that something other than my small consciousness was at work. With both women I journeyed for, I lay down next to them without knowing their question. The first was a woman about thirty-five, a body-worker with long, blonde rippling hair and wide hips. During the journey, Kan showed me the image of a woman's vaginal opening packed with dark, smooth stones. This was such a disconcerting, personal image I wondered if I should even relate it to the stranger beside me. After we sat up, I almost apologetically told her what I had seen. Her eyes teared up as she told me that her question was whether she would ever be able to have children. The doctors had found nothing wrong with her or her husband but she couldn't seem to conceive. She asked me to interpret the image and I was stymied. I told her I was just learning and she needed to interpret for herself, but privately I had the distinct feeling that she would never conceive. She is past childbearing years now and has no children.

For the second woman, slender and green-eyed with a cap of black curls, Kan opened his paw and a large, iridescent butterfly floated out. We consulted my books and found that one of the main attributes of the butterfly is transformation. This seemed to please her, although she didn't tell me her question until months later when she called to relate that she had asked about leaving her verbally abusive husband. The butterfly image had provided the final nudge. She had ended the marriage and was experiencing a transformative change in her life. These connections were fascinating, but the cloak of authority has never wrapped comfortably about my shoulders. I didn't see myself telling seekers what to do with their lives, even if a spiritual force guided me. I knew from reading about other shamanic practitioners that it sometimes took years to become proficient in deciphering these messages from the spirit worlds. Perhaps I didn't really trust the process; perhaps I was just impatient. Whatever the reason, I enjoyed using journeys with Kan as a touchstone to guide the answers to my personal questions.

Kan continues to be a comfort and an inspiration. It is important for me to know he will always be there, waiting in the imaginal world, with his deep, black eyes, his soft, buttery fur and his signature aroma, wind over snow.

The End

www.ingramcontent.com/pod-product-compliance
Lightning Source LLC
Chambersburg PA
CBHW020345260626
47156CB00004B/1683